# WHO CAN YOU TRUST

## A NOVEL

### A'DONNA RENEE

This book is fiction. All names, people, locations, and events are used factiously and are products of the author's imagination.

# TABLE OF CONTENTS

# Chapter 1: SESSION 1... AGAIN

I can't believe I'm here. Sitting in this chair, in my thoughts, staring at this lady, sweating bullets, but, ready to restore the pieces of my life after eight years. I guess it took Daddy's heart attack and running into Travis last year that made me hit my breaking point... at work while operating, trying to save someone when I can't even save myself. Anyway, I still feel embarrassed about that. I thought I hid and buried everything so well, especially at work.

I walked out of the last session. Hopefully, she don't piss me off again this time. Or I will again without hesitation...

"Hi, Dr. Williamson, how are you doing today, in this moment?"

"I told you, you can call me Bianca," I said, sticking my chest out.

"You are right, it's just standard when I speak with the other M.D. 's but I will remember moving forward. How are you? You walked out last session."

"I remember. I'm okay, I guess. Just ready to get back to work." Holding up my hands like a stop sign.

"Look, Dr…" clears throat "Bianca, the only way therapy works is if you work it. I can't force you to share, but I can't sign off on your work release until you have completed the required session hours. So, I encourage you to use your time wisely, or else we will see each other more than you want."

I took a slow, deep breath, closed my eyes, and leaned back toward the ceiling.

"Tell me, what can I do to help you get the most out of today's session?" holding her pen ready to write down exactly what I say.

"Can we do two hours today? Once I start talking, I'm not sure where my thoughts will land, and I want to get the hours over with."

"You are actually my last client for the day, so I can make that work as long as you commit to staying the entire time, no matter how hard it may get." Leaning forward as she crossed her legs, adjusting her posture in an upright position, "and it may get pretty heavy."

I nodded as I blinked slowly and looked at her, my head hung low.

"Great. We can jump right in because I sense you have much to say. Let's start from where we left off last week. Tell me about your earliest childhood memory, and we can work on what brought you here, or at least brought you back."

I sat up in the chair and slowly swallowed a big gulp of saliva. I could feel my heart beating fast as I mustered the courage to talk. I grabbed the journal I brought with me and held it close to me like a security blanket.

"My earliest childhood memory goes back to 4th grade in the 1990s at Paul Public Elementary School... deep in the south side of Chicago." I closed my eyes to recreate the memory I had of the neighborhood. "It had rows of brick buildings, dirt as grass and cracked sidewalks, and a school system fighting an uphill battle, but I loved school, especially my 4th grade teacher, Ms. Jefferies. I used to sit eagerly in the front of the class, waiting for her to call my name."

'Bianca Williamson.' Almost as if she were singing my name. I would raise my hand so high, showing all of my teeth, waving my hand internally yelling 'Pick me, Pick me.'"

"Is this the year you met your best friends?" she asked as she jotted down notes.

"Yes. Stephanie and Tia." I avoided eye contact and shrank into myself.

"Bianca, it's okay, you are in therapy for healing, not to be judged. Tell me more about what you remember from 4th grade."

I began to rub my clammy palms together and took a deep breath as I braced myself to tap into the very thing I wanted to put behind me, my past.

## Chapter 2: THE BESTIES

"My best friends Stephanie and Tia loved attending school every day, and we loved learning because of Ms. Jefferies. She stood at the front of the classroom, the kind of woman whose presence could hush a room without raising her voice. Small-framed but commanding, she wore her wisdom like a tailored suit. Her skin was a deep, smooth brown, and her eyes, patient but piercing, held the kind of calm that only years of teaching could carve.

"One day, like every day, her pants hovered just above her polished knee-high stockings. We used to whisper theories about her wardrobe. Some said she wore boots underneath, others insisted it was just part of her mysterious 'teacher swag.' But the truth came out whenever she sat down; her slacks would ride up ever so slightly, revealing the soft tops of her stockings. No boots. Just a woman with her own style and the authority to own it."

As I slowly opened my eyes and stared at the wall, I suddenly remembered one particular weekend that year.

*"Two more minutes to finish your homework. If you're done early, check your answers or, better yet, help someone who is stuck."*

*My hand shot up as usual. I made direct eye contact with Ms. Jefferies, smiling, ready to ask yet another question on behalf of myself and my peers.*

*"Ms. Jefferies, if my test scores show you we did good—I mean, well on the test, can we have free time Monday?"*

*Before Ms. Jefferies could respond, Tia jumped out of her seat like a bottle of soda about to explode, "Naw man, let's have a party! I'ma wear my best outfit, my dookie shirts, and my crop top to show off my stomach."*

Later, she told me that she dressed like her mother and started to behave as if they were equal, partly because when her mother wasn't home, her dad treated her as such. She was responsible for cooking, cleaning, and fulfilling his sexual desires when forced. I learned it wasn't vanity she aimed for; it was survival disguised as confidence. Growing up faster meant gaining control. She was the kind of child who knew how to make herself seen, even if she often felt invisible deep down.

*"We could have free time outside and a party. That way,*

everybody would be pleased," Stephanie chimed in with a smile and folded her hands as if the case was closed and solved the mystery, then grabbed some snacks from her desk. She was always snacking on something.

Ms. Jefferies shook her head slowly. "No, we are not going to have free time, nor are we going to have a party. Scanning the room as each child's head hung low.

"But I can bring cupcakes the day after the test, and during snack time, I can pass them out with some of the school milk." Tia groaned and smacked her lips.

"Or," Ms. Jefferies warned, "I can bring nothing."

A chorus of voices rose in protest. "No, no! Cupcakes, please!"

"Okay," Ms. Jefferies said, regaining control. "Well, you all need to control yourselves. But we've wasted too much time on irrelevant things. We have less than a minute to leave. I want everyone to be quiet as you pack up your belongings."

I leaned over as everyone packed up and whispered to my friends.
"Hey, you two wanna spend the night at my house this weekend? We can have a girl's night and study for the test on Monday." Ms. Jefferies caught me in the act.

*"Um, Bianca, I know you're not being disruptive. You know your parents wouldn't be happy if I had to make a phone call." My face turned red as she lowered her gaze. "It won't happen again."*

*"You're right. It won't happen again. Monday, I'm switching seats. People will no longer be around their friends during school again. Look at the time, time to go. Make sure you all study!"*

*"You need to pass, and I know we all want those cupcakes!" I said playfully as we filed out of the classroom one by one.*

*"Bye class, see you all at school on Monday. Have a great weekend."*

*"Bye, Ms. Jefferies!"*

Stephanie, Tia, and I always walked home from school together for safety. That day, we walked shoulder to shoulder, the biting Chicago wind tugging at our coats like impatient hands. It was supposed to be spring, but the air felt more like the middle of winter, sharp, gray, and unapologetically cold. Our breath came out in visible clouds, and our steps quickened as we made our way down the cracked sidewalk. Around us, other students were still bundled up in thick hats, knit scarves, and oversized gloves, their laughter laced with shivers. Despite the chill, we talked and laughed as we always did, our closeness creating a warmth that the weather couldn't touch.

*"So, do you want to spend the night at my house?" I asked again, "we can study, hang out, and talk about boys. Did you see Travis today? He is so cute. He will be my husband one day, just watch. He has the best smile and the perfect brown skin.*

*"Yes!" said Stephanie as she clapped her hands together, "I just have to call my mom. She will say yes. I saw Travis, and he wasn't paying you no mind Bianca. Titling her head to the side attempting to convince me."*

*"YES he was! He was looking right at me the entire day." I said laughing loudly.*

*Tia's face fell, and her smile faded as quickly as it had come. "Naw, I can't." she whispered, "I have to watch my little brother and sister. My mom has to work all weekend."*

Her mother was *always* working. Sixteen-hour days were routine, cycling between jobs that barely paid enough to keep the lights on. Most nights, she came home just long enough to eat, shower, and collapse for a couple of hours before heading right back out. There were no weekends, no breaks, just survival.

*"Really? You always have to watch them. Why can't your dad do it? He makes you do everything Tia!" smacking my lips.*

*Tia sighed, kicking at a pebble on the sidewalk. "I know. But my mom says it's part of growing up. And my dad... he says he doesn't wanna be bothered with them because they cry too much."*

*"Well, how about you bring your brother and sister over for the weekend again? That way, we can all still be together. Is that okay, Bianca? And will your parents say yes too?"*

*"Yes, I guess," I turn my head away from the conversation.*

I was the only child, so I didn't understand Tia's responsibilities fully.

*Tia began to smile and jumped up and down. "Okay, that sounds great! I can't wait to come over. All we have to do is pack our clothes. Thank you again, Bianca. My brother and sister will be so happy. They love coming to your house."*

*"No problem,"* in a low mumbling tone as I rolled my eyes.

*"We'll meet you halfway in 30 minutes to help with all the bags."*

*"Okay!"*

"I hoped this time would be just the three of us because Tia always had to bring her siblings every time she came over." But the three of us parted ways when we reached the end of the block, unaware of how deeply the weekend ahead would change all of our lives."

"How was Tia's upbringing? Did she ever share any details about that weekend with you? Would you like to share that?"

"Sure. That was the weekend that changed everything."
I inhaled deeply and exhaled so loud I could blow out a candle from a mile away.

"I only went to Tia's apartment once. From what I could remember, it was dim and weary. She shared with me several times how she hated going home. It wasn't until we were adults that Tia explicitly told me what was going on. She remembered every detail so vividly that it was almost like she was reliving the situation all over again."

I opened the journal I found at her apartment eight years ago and began to read what was written.

## Chapter 3: BEHIND TIA'S DOORS

When I was a child, my apartment was dim and weary, the walls echoing the weight of neglect and abuse. I hated going home. One day, after school, my shoulders stiffened from the responsibility I bore at just ten years old. Derrick was sprawled on the couch, a permanent fixture of disinterest and irritation. I haven't called him daddy since I ran away.

Derrick was the kind of man whose charm wore thin the closer you stood to him. From a distance, he carried himself with the type of swagger that drew attention, shoulders back, head high, voice loud. He talked like he had the world figured out and had answers for problems he never tried to solve. But behind the confidence was a deep-rooted immaturity that festered in someone who never truly grew up.

He had no desire to work hard or work at all. Labor, in his mind, was someone else's burden. While others woke up early, juggled schedules, and pushed through exhaustion, Derrick spent his days pacing the house, yelling at the news, complaining about the system, and blaming the world for dreams he never pursued. He was loud, reactive, and entitled.

To keep his wife, my mama, happy or at least silent, he manipulated the home into performing stability. When Mama got home from another double shift, Derrick would lean against the doorway and take the credit, spinning lies with a smile while I stood silently in the background, too afraid to contradict him.

Eventually, Mama gave up the fantasy of Derrick ever becoming a provider. She stopped begging him to get a job and pushing him to lead. Instead, she took on the weight herself, working sixteen-hour days just to keep the lights on, pretending not to notice her husband's laziness and manipulations. To her, losing her man was worse than losing herself. So she stayed and she worked.

Derrick didn't just fail as a father, he failed as a man. He distorted my understanding of love, trust, and masculinity. And though he was often idle, his presence was heavy looming in the house like a warning no one could speak aloud. His absence might have been easier to survive. But his existence was a quiet undoing of everyone around him.

*"Hey Dad, is Mama here?" I avoided all eye contact and looked down.*

*Derrick didn't even turn his head. "Do you see your mama around here? I'm tryna rest. Them kids been crying all damn day. Go see what's wrong with them."*

*My 5-year-old siblings, Stacey and Stanley, whines carried from the other room like sirens that I couldn't ignore.*

*They were more like my children. The responsibility I carried for them ran deeper than chores, it was maternal, instinctive, and far beyond what any child should've had to bear. They respected me not just as a sister, but as the most stable figure in their world. When I left for school each morning, they'd cling to my legs or whimper quietly from the couch, dreading the hours without me. My absence meant they had to fend for themselves, even at just five years old. I knew this because this was how our weekends were, fending for ourselves.*

*"What's wrong?" kneeling beside them.*

*"We hungry," they answered in unison, rubbing their eyes.*

*I turned back toward the living room. "Dad, they said they're hungry."*

*"Then fix 'em something!"* Derrick snapped, finally sitting up, *"why are you tellin' me? Find something for them rugrats to eat! Don't ask me no dumb questions!"*

*"Yes sir,"* I replied softly and moved to the kitchen.

*I began opening cabinets, searching for anything I could make. The kitchen was half-empty, and the pantry was stocked only with canned goods and scattered boxes. Behind me, I remember Stanley wandering in.*

*"Tia, can you make me some chicken?"* he asked with chips crumbs all over his face.

*My patience cracked.*

*"LOOK! I barely know how to cook. I'm gonna make what I know how to make. Just go in the room and I'll bring it to you soon!"*

*My outburst brought Derrick thundering in from the couch.*

*"Tia, you ain't got no kids around here! Stop yellin' at them like they yours before I whoop you."*

*All I said was "okay."*

*"Who the hell you sayin' 'okay' to?" he roared, "It's yes SIR! Get in the room. Assume the position!"*

*"But Dad, please—"*

*"You talkin' back? That's double. GO TO THE ROOM!"*

*The twins cried again as they scurried away, the confusion and fear etched on their small faces. Derrick turned to them. "Y'all ain't that hungry. She'll feed you in a minute. Get them chips and go sit down."*

My heart pounded as I walked into the bedroom, tears already streaking down my face. Outside, the day continued like any other. But inside, time stopped for me. Carrying burdens far too heavy. He often found things to get mad at me about and then "punished" me. This was his way of justifying his actions. This had been going on for as long as I could remember, at least since I was about eight or nine.

## Chapter 4: THE SECRET WEIGHT

Tia's voice trembled as she whispered into the receiver when I spoke to her that night, her words shaky and wet with tears.

*"Yeah… I don't think I can come over."*

*"Why not?"* My voice was cautious, laced with worry, *"It happened again?*

*… "Yes."*

I remember taking a deep, long sigh and saying. *"Tia, you need to tell your mother. Do you need me to come over to talk to him?"*

I was known for always advocating for my friends.

*"Bianca, I can't tell her again. She already knows, trust me. I tried before, and she whooped me. Told me if I ever come to her with something she doesn't want to hear again, she's gonna knock my head off my shoulders."*

"Dang... well, I wouldn't tell her either," I muttered, "but, you can tell the police. They won't knock your head off your shoulders."

"This ain't funny," Tia snapped, "and I hope you didn't tell Stephanie all my business either. I don't want her trying to take up for both of us."

"Come on now, you know me better than that," "You know I would never do you like that. Anything she knows, it's because you told her."

"Good," Tia said flatly. "Then she don't know anything."

"So, what are you going to do? You don't need to keep going through this."

"I don't know. I have to figure something out. This is too hard," Tia broke down, her voice barely holding together, "I don't like it when my brother and sister see me cry like this. I have to be strong for them. Why does it have to happen to me? I know this is all my fault. I know it is."

"Tia, it is not your fault," I often said firmly.

*"I just don't know what to do. I want to tell, but I'm too scared. But I don't want to end up pregnant. All that stuff we learned in health... it really scared me."*

*"None of this is your fault. And yes, we learned all that stuff in health class. Something could happen. You should tell someone so he doesn't do it again."*

*"I know... I just don't want nothing to happen to my daddy and then my mama be mad at me. I'm just.. I don't know. I wish I could run away like the people on TV. Or I wish this had happened to somebody else. You and Stephanie live perfect lives. And—"*

*"Tia, we don't live perfect lives. Stuff happens to me too just not the same stuff. Look, you, your brother, and sister need to sneak out and come live with us. My parents love kids and always wanted more."* As I paced my room trying to figure out how to help my friend.

*"I don't know about living, but when my dad goes to sleep in about fifteen minutes, I can get the twins and leave. He sleeps hard and goes fast, so he won't hear a thing. We'll talk to your parents. I'll make up a story so they don't ask too many questions."*

"Okay, "Stephanie and I will meet you at the corner. Be there."

"Thank you. You are the best thing that's ever happened to me. And Stephanie, too. Without y'all… I don't know what I'd do. Y'all two are the only ones I can trust."

"That's what friends are for." And we hung up.

\*\*\*

When I heard Derrick go back to the couch, I moved slowly toward my closet quietly, as if each step weighed more than the last. My fingers trembled as I reached for the bottom drawer, the one I kept hidden beneath clothes I never wore. Buried beneath layers of denial and quiet panic was a small, pink box worn at the edges from being handled too many times.

A pregnancy test.

My mama had bought it for me after the last scare. Not out of care, but out of avoidance. A quiet solution to a louder problem she refused to face. '*Just in case*,' my mama had said. There was only one left.

I took it with me into the bathroom, locking the door behind me with a click that felt final. The small space was filled with the

24

sound of my breath, shallow and uneven. I set the box on the sink and stared at it for a long time, wishing it would disappear. Wishing I could disappear so I wouldn't feel anymore.

I followed the instructions mechanically. I had done this before. More times than a ten-year-old should ever know how to. I waited, clutching the counter with both hands, eyes fixed on the floor. The seconds dragged on each one pressing against my chest like a weight.

The window was no longer blank when I finally looked down at the test.

Two faint pink lines.

My knees buckled and I sank to the floor, clutching my stomach as I cried.

*"Tia! Shut the hell up in there!" Derrick's voice thundered through the house.*

 I jumped, wiping my tears away, walked swiftly out of the bathroom and into my room to my desk. Silently, I opened my school notebook and began to write:

*Mom,*

*I can't stay in this house. You always at work and don't what's going on here. Dad don't take care of the twins they only eat*

*when I feed them. I told you what is being done to me, and you don't listen. I hate coming to this house and I hate seeing my brother and sister go through this. I am running away and never coming back. If you look for us, I will tell the police everything. Since you are never here anyway, you won't miss us. Don't worry I will make sure Stacey and Stanley are okay. But we need to get out of this house.*

*Bye.*

*P.S. I took a pregnancy test. It got two lines.*

I folded the note carefully and placed it on my desk. Then, I began stuffing clothes into a backpack.

Suddenly, Stacey peeked in through the cracked door

*"Tia, Mommy's home."*

*"What? Where is she?"*

*"In the room talking to Daddy."*

*My heart dropped. I tossed the bag into the closet and tried to calm my breathing. Moments later, the bedroom door opened.*

26

*Mama's voice rang out, sharp and accusatory. "So I heard you weren't listening and trying to be fast, huh? And why is this phone in here?*

*"I wasn't trying to be fast," I lied, "I was calling Stephanie to get help with homework because I was in the bathroom when the teacher explained it."*

*Mama narrowed her eyes. "Yo period still ain't come?"*

*"No."*

*"When was your last one?"*

*"January. Two months ago. Mama, I took the test. The one we already had.... It got two lines."*

*Mama froze. "You better not have told anybody."*

*"No, Mama. I didn't."*

*"I'm calling the doctor tomorrow. You better not tell a soul. If anyone asks, you were raped but you don't know who did it. Understand?"*

*"Yes, ma'am."*

*"Where's the test?"*

*"In the bathroom trash."*

*Mama stormed into the bathroom and retrieved it. "Damn! Always something with you. I can't even look at you right now."*

*She left and headed straight for Derrick.*

*"She took the test."*

*"So?" as Derrick stared at the television, half asleep on the couch.*

*"She's pregnant." Slamming the test on the couch.*

*"How the hell is she pregnant? She's ten!" he sat up to look at the test.*

*"She's got a period and she's having sex. What do you expect?"*

*"Well, y'all should've told me something. What y'all gonna do? She told anybody?"*

*"No. I'm calling the doctor in the morning. We'll just say she got raped."*

*"You better hope it works. I'm not going to jail. I didn't know she started her period. Now I gotta use rubbers. Might as well just sleep with you."*

*Mama rolled her eyes and grabbed her purse. "I need to run to the store. I'll be back."*

*"Take those kids with you. I ain't been able to rest all day, shit I'm tired."*

*"I'll be quicker without them. I'll hurry back." She slammed the door shut.*

*Soon after Derrick fell asleep, I crept to the twins room, "Stacey. Stanley. Shhh. Get your shoes. Grab that bag. We're leaving."*

*"Okay." In unison, they stumbled over their shoes, clothes, and broken toys as they got dressed and headed to the door with their bag.*

*Stacey dropped her bag, and it thudded against the floor.*

*I froze, then whispered, "It's okay. Just keep moving. I got it."*

*With my heart pounding, I locked the front door behind them.*

We never looked back after this day. We ran away to Bianca's house for the weekend, and Derrick was in jail by that Sunday. He was sentenced to twenty years for abuse, rape and child neglect.

Mama had called to make me an appointment, and after the questionnaire, DCFS made a trip to my house and Bianca's house. Derrick and Mama tried to lie, but they saw right through it. Mama didn't get caught because she blamed it on being at work and not knowing what was happening.

My siblings blamed me when they got older and hadn't talked to me since. After several attempts, I gave up and decided to wait for them to seek me. But they never did…

Even still, I was so lucky to have Bianca's family take my siblings and me in. That was the best day of my life.

## Chapter 5: STEPHANIE'S EYES

"Stephanie, you have been teaching here for the past 8 years, but I still don't know anything about you, " said Ms. Jefferies.

"I don't talk much about my past. It's not one I am fond of."

"Well, we all have skeletons in our closets. I may come in my tailored suit ready to teach, but my life hasn't been filled with rainbows either. "

"I tell you what, you share a few of your fondest memories and I will share mine."

"You know you have been negotiating every single conversation since you were in my class," she chuckled, that's a good trait to always keep with you. Deal."

Even though I always tried to compromise, it was never a strength of mine. It never really went my way.

"One weekend, Bianca, Tia, and I walked home from school, and we talked about going to Bianca's house that night for the weekend. I hadn't even asked my mother yet. I just knew I was going… I stood in the living room, gathering my things for the night ahead. I told my mother I was heading to Bianca's house to study for the big test.

I grew up in a stable, faith-driven home, where church on Sundays was as regular as school on Mondays. My parents weren't rich, but they were loving, steadfast in discipline, overflowing with scripture, and constantly reminding me that God doesn't make mistakes. It was a message I carried, clung to, and sometimes used like armor when the world didn't make sense.

*My mother, Mrs. Richards, sat with gentle eyes but concern in her voice. "Maybe the three of you can all make it to church on Sunday?" she suggested.*

*I politely declined, knowing my friends weren't as deeply involved in church life as my family. Tension rose briefly as her mother mentioned Natalie, a more churchgoing girl.*

*Mother sighed. "Why don't you spend more time with friends like Natalie? She's more into church."*

*"Because she's boring, Mom," I said bluntly.*

*Mother's face dropped as she quirked her eyebrows together.*

*"Let me pick your friends and you pick mine?"*

*"Excuse me?" snapping her neck and putting her hand on her hip.*

*"Nothing."*

*"That's what I thought I heard. What time are you leaving? Will you be gone before your dad gets off?"*

*"Actually, I'm leaving in about 30 minutes, so I will see Dad tomorrow."*

Dad, Pastor Richards, was a well-respected pastor in their community. He embodied a Godly man to the outside world: articulate, powerful in the pulpit, and always ready with scripture on his tongue.

But behind the pulpit, the picture wasn't quite so holy. While the Pastor spent most of his time at the church preaching, teaching, and "serving the Lord" there were whispers. Quiet ones. Rumors crept through the pews like drafts on a cold Sunday morning. It wasn't uncommon for him to stay long after service, often under the guise of counseling a troubled female member. The stories changed depending on who you asked, but the pattern was always the same.

Mother found out about his infidelity just before I was born. It wasn't just one woman it had been several, over several years. I had discovered a trail of betrayal tucked between church bulletins, "emergency prayer meetings," and long nights that ended in excuses. But she didn't leave.

Maybe it was pride, maybe it was pressure, maybe it was the church culture that taught women to "stand by their man" no matter the storm. Whatever it was, she continued to bury her heartbreak beneath layers of grace and grit.

Those seeds of contradiction planted something in me early: a deep commitment to truth, loyalty, and living right. I didn't want to be like Dad, loved by many but faithful to none. I didn't want to become like Mother, either strong but silenced by sacrifice. Unfortunately, a part of each of them was already instilled in me.

## Chapter 6: THE MEET UP

Later, the three of us met at the corner. Our parents didn't mind me being outside alone. As harsh as the neighborhood was, everyone treated each other like family.

Stephanie looked down at Tia's large bags.

*"Why do you have so many?"*

*"Oh... no reason. The twins mess their clothes up a lot. I brought extras."*

Stephanie teased, *"I thought you were running away or something."*

Tia did a two-chuckle laugh. *"Oh no!"* *"Why would I be running away?"*

*"I don't know,"* Stephanie said, shrugging, *"why do you do a lot of things?"*

*"A lot of things like what?"* Tia snapped.

*"Nothing. Forget I said anything."*

*I stepped between them. "Tia. Stephanie. Please..." Then turned to the twins. "Hey, babies!"*

*"Hi," they chirped.*

*"Okay, Tia, give me one of your bags so we can go." Changing the subject.*

As we walked down the block, I could see the weight of secrets pressed heavily on Tia's small shoulders. She was distracted, barely engaging in conversation and asking us to repeat ourselves.

*When they arrived back at my house, I took them upstairs quickly. I glanced behind me and saw that my mom gave Tia a warm, yet slightly curious, glance. The twins were shy but delighted by the sight of the cozy house and the smell of real food. I had already informed her mom that Tia's mom had to work, so the twins would stay the night. They were okay with this. I didn't tell her the details because I avoided things like that.*

My parents were loving and hardworking, the kind of people who sacrificed quietly and prayed loudly. They hadn't had much education themselves, barely making it through high school, but they believed in its power with the conviction of people who had once lived without it. And so they poured that belief into me, reminding me often that knowledge wasn't just opportunity, it was freedom.

My dad's relationship with my mother was the kind of relationship people admired quietly, steadily, affectionately, and really. They laughed often and loved loudly, never hiding their tenderness. Hugs in the kitchen, inside jokes across the dinner table. He still opened the door for her, still called her "mama" with a wink when annoyed, and still danced with her in the living room to old-school R&B just because it was Tuesday.

After my mother had cooked my favorite dinner, meatloaf with string beans and garlic mashed potatoes, she came to check in on us in my room.

*"I know your girlfriends are here, but let's not forget the main reason: two hours of studying."*

*I groaned, "2?"*

*"Or no company?"*

*With displeasure, I said, "Fine, 2 hours."*

*"Good! I knew you would come to your senses. Your dad will be in the living room, and I will be in the kitchen if you need us" as she exited my room.*

My father was a man you noticed the moment he entered a room not just because of his 6'0", 280-pound frame, but because of the warmth that followed him like a second skin. With oil-stained hands, a deep baritone laugh, and a face that always seemed on the verge of a smile, he was the kind of man who could fix a car engine with one hand and wipe away his daughter's tears with the other.

Daddy came in to say hi to us. It was his way to show "he was cool".

*"What's going on, girls? What ya'll got planned for the evening? Nails?" as he laughed, holding out his hands, mimicking us.*

*"Dad! Please!"*

*"Alright, alright I leave you all to it. When you get to the toes, let me know. I need a pedicure! As he walked out closing the door.*

*"Your dad is so funny B. I wish my daddy hung out with me like your dad." Said Stephanie.*

*"Yeah, he is pretty cool. We always hang out."*

*Tia's face hung low as she bit her nails.*

Everyone settled in quickly. After dinner, we studied together as promised. I kept checking the clock while Stephanie scribbled notes. Tia remained quiet, doing her best to focus.

She said her mind kept replaying everything her father's rage, her mother's denial, the pregnancy test. But when the studying ended, Tia finally breathed a sigh of relief. That night, the three of us laughed softly in the dark, the twins asleep nearby.

*"Travis is so cute," I said in a blushing tone.*

*"Oh my God, B, why don't you just say something to him tomorrow?" Stephanie replied.*

*"I will. But what do you think he will say? He's always talking low and smiling. Did you see his dimples? He's so smart too."*

*"Girl, I ignore him. My mind stays on Jesus! We will just have to wait until tomorrow and see what he says."*

Both of us laughed more and felt like everything was okay, and for a moment, it felt like things might be okay with Tia.

"That seems like the turning point in all of your lives, would you agree?" as she waited for me so she could write down the answer.

Twirling my hair, looking out the window, "Yeah, I would like to think so."

"Would you like to discuss more?"

"Not about my childhood. I'm over it."

I was known for avoiding things that cause me to over-explain or feel guilty about something.

"Okay, let's discuss college?" as she turned the page of her notepad.

## Chapter 7: 12 YEARS LATER

Twelve years had passed since the night Tia ran away with her little brother and sister. Twelve years since the screams, secrets, and silence of abuse.

Now, she stood in her small apartment off-campus. The girl who had once lived in fear was now a woman: still strong, still scarred, and still trying to believe that strength was enough.

In the living room, Stephanie and I sat cross-legged on the floor, surrounded by textbooks, lemonade, and snacks, and laughter that was beginning to fade. The evening had started with warmth, but something unspoken hung in the air, like a thunderstorm waiting just beyond the skyline.

*"Man, class this morning was so stressful. I hate this med class!"* Flopping back onto a throw pillow, *"I could barely pay attention. I'm just ready to finish at SU, marry Travis, and start my real life."* I smiled, a dreamy, hopeful kind of smile that belonged to a woman with her life mapped out.

*"Marriage. Career. Family."* Stephanie chuckled.

"Girl, I don't know how you handle all those science courses. I'd have snapped by now."

"Thinking about what's next keeps me going," twirling a pen in my hand.

"Dr. Bianca Jamerson. Sounds good, right?"

"It does. And when those kids at school are sick, I'm sending them straight to you." Mrs. Jamerson, huh?" Stephanie jokingly said.

"You got that right. Travis says it sounds perfect, and we can't wait to make it official. I can't believe we have been together for four years already, and now marriage! I remember being mesmerized by the smallest things he did in fourth grade. I thought I was so in love. But I remember telling y'all he will be my husband," chuckling, waving my engagement ring in the air.

"It's funny how college has brought us back together after he transferred after fourth grade. I would've never thought in a million years."

"I know that's right. I'm so proud of you! I still can't believe *how small this world is. Who would've thought you two would reconnect freshman year? The same college, same campus, same dorm building! That's insane."*

*"Girl, tell me about it," I said, as my cheeks began to turn pale, showing my teeth.*

*"But I'm still a little upset that Tia said she couldn't attend the wedding. What did she say she had to do again?" she asked, puzzled.*

*"She claims she is going out of town with her siblings. I didn't even know they were talking again."*

*"They are? I didn't know that either." I crossed my legs and leaned into the couch's arm, my voice tinged with suspicion and frustration.*

*"Yeah, that's what she told me," I muttered, swirling the condensation on my glass with a fingertip. "But it's kind of funny, don't you think? She and the twins just so happen to go on vacation on the exact same weekend as my wedding? Come on. I'm not dumb."*

*Stephanie looked up from her notebook, concerned. "Bianca..."*

*"I'm not going to say anything," I interrupted, brushing a strand of hair behind my ear. "I'll let her have her little vacation, I'm going to be the bigger person. But you and I both know how she is. She's always had issues with other people being happy. Always been the jealous type."*

*Stephanie narrowed her eyes, "Bianca, that's our best friend. You know she'd be devastated if she heard you say that. The Bible says, 'Judge not, that ye be not judged.'"*

*I let out a sharp breath and rolled my eyes. "Okay, "preacher", but you know I'm right. It's the truth, and you've seen it, too."*

*"Yeah... You're right. It is the truth. But that's just how she is. Either we keep accepting it, or we say something."*

*"Well, you already know I'm not afraid to confront anyone, especially not someone I consider family. If I can't call out my friends, who can I?"*

*"We've been putting up with her behavior for twelve years," Stephanie said, half-shrugging, "at this point, it's second nature. We've just learned to live with it."*

*I leaned and whispered, "and that's exactly the problem. We've been enabling it. I'm tired of the jealousy. I'm tired of walking on eggshells. And don't pretend like you're not tired of it too, Steph."*

*Stephanie looked down, "she doesn't always mean it," her words cracked.*

*I threw my hands up and down, slamming them onto the couch. "That's just another excuse. You know what I think? I think the reason she acts like this is because she's alone. No man. No one to love her. And deep down, she probably wishes she had my life."*

*Stephanie didn't respond.*

*My phone rang.*

*"Hey, Fiancé! You are on speaker."*

*"Hey, baby, how are you doing? Hey, everybody over there."*

Travis made me smile every time I spoke to him. The idea of starting my life with he man of my dreams was so liberating.

*"I'm blessed and highly favored," Stephanie said, holding her hands to her heart.*

*"Tia's in the restroom, but I will tell her you said hello baby."*

*"Okay, cool. I wanted to check in and see what you wanted for dinner. You may be too tired when you get home to cook, so I will pick up something or cook my favorite dish you like."*

*"Oh, baby, you are so thoughtful. I am open to whatever."*

*"That is so sweet! You go Travis!" Stephanie said, clapping her hands.*

*"Okay, Mrs. Jamerson," as he laughed softly. I love you, baby."*

*"I love you too Mr. Jamerson. Bye."*

Tia, who had just stepped out of the bathroom, overheard us discussing the wedding planning earlier and felt the air shift when she entered.

*"And when are y'all gonna stop talking about this damn wedding?" she snapped, drying her arms with the towel. "It's not until 100 years from now." rolling her eyes and sucking her teeth.*

*"Okay? What's with the attitude? Are you jealous or something? It's not 100 years, it's in 1 year."*

*Tia's jaw tightened. "Why would I be jealous?"*

*"Exactly what I'm asking," I said, eyes narrowing.*

*"You always do this. You act happy for me, but the minute I talk about anything good in my life, you change the subject or start throwing shade."*

*"Hey, hey, come on. Let's not fight."*

*"Shut up, Stephanie," Tia shot back. "You always playing peacekeeper. It's annoying."*

*Stephanie stood up.*

*"No. Not this time. You need to hear this, Tia. Bianca is our best friend. We're supposed to celebrate her, not make her feel bad for being happy."*

*Tia's voice rose, her emotions spilling out like a dam finally breaking. "You two have always been against me!" she shouted, standing rigid in the middle of the room, "It was always 'Bianca and Stephanie. Never Tia. I always had to get in where I fit in, like I was the extra. Like, I didn't belong. I couldn't say or do anything without it turning into a damn problem."*

*Stephanie's eyes widened. "That's not true! I treat everyone equally, Tia. Always have. God said, 'So whatever you wish that others would do to you, do also to them, for this is the Law and the Prophets.' I live by that. If I were against you, I would've told..."*

*"Stephanie!" Tia barked, eyes wide with panic.*

*"Would've told what?" as I slowly turned my head, looking at both of them.*

*Tia looked away. "Nothing. Just leave it alone."*

*"No," I yelled. "Somebody better tell me something. Right now."*

*The room went still, the tension so thick it could've been cut with a knife. What had started as an argument now teetered on the edge of revelation, one that could shatter them all.*

*Stephanie glanced nervously at Tia, her face was red, and her hands shook uncontrollably. Tia's eyes darted between her friends, one full of betrayal, the other full of fear. Her clammy fists clenched at her sides, trying to stop her hands from shaking.*

*"Tia, what is going on?" Tia's breath was uneven. Her gaze finally landed on me, and her voice trembled, not from fear, but from rage that had fermented into bitterness.*

*"You want to know?" she said, "Fine!" She swallowed hard, then dropped the truth like a blade between them.*

*"I've been messing around with Travis, for the past three years."*

*I didn't move, didn't blink. The words didn't register at first; they floated like heavy smoke, choking.*

*"What?" I whispered.*

*Tia's voice was flat now, emotionless. "You heard me."*

*Stephanie stepped back, her face pale, her mouth slightly open. My breath caught in my throat. "My Travis?" I asked, my voice shaking.*

*"How many Travis's do you know?" Tia replied coldly.*

*I turned to Stephanie slowly, her voice sharp with betrayal. "You knew?"*

*Stephanie opened her mouth, but no words came out.*

*"I said, you knew?"*

*Stephanie nodded helplessly, shame clouding her face.*

*The silence between them exploded like shattered glass. I took a step back, my heart pounding.*

*"You're both dead to me and the wedding is off," I whispered. I didn't scream. I didn't cry. I simply turned, walked to the door, and left.*

*"But Bianca! I already bought my dress!"*

*"Wear it in Hell!"*

And in my absence, the weight of everything that had gone wrong in their friendship settled across the room like ash after a fire.

## Chapter 8: THE BLAME GAME

Our friendship began to fall apart after I told B about Tia and Travis. I remember how Tia stared at the closed door for a long moment before rounding on me. Her eyes blazed with fury.

*"Now look what you did. You couldn't keep your mouth shut, could you? You just had to let it slip."*

*My entire body jumped. "What I did? Tia, you're the one who slept with her fiancé. Don't try to put this on me."*

*"You don't get it," Tia hissed, pacing now, "I was going to end it. Eventually, once the wedding actually happened, I was going to stop. I didn't want to keep hurting her."*

*Folding my arms, "That makes it better?"*

*"It makes it manageable!" as the veins popped out of her neck, "and what did you do? You just outed me like you were waiting for the perfect chance."*

*"It slipped out, I didn't mean to. But you've been putting me in the middle of this for three years. What did you expect?"*

Tia squinted her eyes, "You had no problem keeping the secret before."

"Because I didn't want to lose either of you!" my voice cracked, "I thought if I stayed quiet, maybe it would go away. But it didn't. It just got worse. And you... You just kept digging the hole deeper."

"Oh, so now you're the victim? You were just as complicit. Guilty by association."

"Maybe. But I never betrayed her. You did."

Tia's lips curled bitterly, "you talk so much about right and wrong, but you watched me struggle all these years and never once asked why. You never asked why I did what I did."

"I don't need to know why you did it, all I know is that it hurt her. And it wasn't just a mistake. It was a choice. Over and over again."

Tia looked away, her jaw clenched. Her voice dropped, quieter but full of venom. "People have done way worse to me. You think I've had it easy? You think I don't know what betrayal feels like?"

*"That's not what this is about. This isn't about your past, Tia. It's about what you did to the one person who never stopped defending you."*

*Tia turned her back, unable to respond.*

*I gathered my things. The weight of the argument had drained me. "You need help, Tia. And I don't mean a lecture. I mean real help. Someone to talk to. Because the way you keep burning bridges, one day there won't be anyone left."*

*"Get out of my house," Tia said without turning around.*

*"I'm praying for you," I said softly, "whether you want it or not."*

*I left, and Tia stood alone in her living room, surrounded by silence and betrayal.*

Ms. Jefferies stood with her mouth wide open. "Wow! I did not anticipate such a memory! I mean, I was expecting you to tell me about a tragedy because of your demeanor at work every day, but this takes the cake."

"That's not even half the story," I said as I stacked my papers.

## Chapter 9: THE BREAKING POINT

***

The sky outside had turned an ashen gray. Clouds hung low, heavy with the weight of a coming storm. I sat in my apartment, barely breathing, as the silence pressed in around me like a vice. Every memory of Travis, the laughter, the late-night talks, the quiet kisses, suddenly felt tainted.

I didn't just fall in love with Travis, I fell in love with who he was becoming. The first time we reconnected after 12 years, freshman year in college, he spoke with such clarity and conviction about his future that it was impossible not to be drawn in. He had a plan: law school, a courtroom, and a mission to fight for justice. He wasn't just smart but sharp, articulate, and passionate. He carried a leather-bound planner, kept color-coded notebooks, and quoted court cases like most guys quoted rappers.

I was already driven and drawn to his ambition like a moth to a flame. We would sit up late talking about the future, mine in medicine, his in law. We promised each other success and swore we'd be the power couple everyone envied. He sold me the dream, and I believed in it not just because it was beautiful, but because it was him. His confidence made it feel real.

The front door creaked open.

*"Hey baby!" Travis called as he stepped inside, keys jingling in his hand, and Chinese food in his hand. "How were classes today, you need a foot rub again?"*

*I stood still, arms folded, eyes locked on him with quiet fury.*

*Travis slowly put everything down on the table, staring at me. "Everything alright?"*

*"You tell me, as I walked towards him, "you and Tia have been messing around for three years?"*

*Travis blinked, stumbling as he took a step backwards, "What?"*

*"Don't play dumb with me, I know. I know everything. And don't you dare lie."*

*He scratched the back of his head, suddenly avoiding my stare. "Okay... okay, yeah," he admitted, the words spilling out like poison, but it wasn't supposed to happen like this. I wasn't even into her like that at first, I swear."*

*I laughed, sharp and humorless. "Three years, Travis. That's not a slip-up. That's a second relationship."*

*"I didn't mean to hurt you," stepping closer, "you were always busy, school, work, always gone. I felt... I don't know... alone."*

*"So, you went to my best friend?" as my voice bounced off the walls, "The girl who was practically family?"*

*His lips trembled, "Baby, it didn't mean anything. You're the one I want. She was just... a distraction."*

*"A. distraction. You proposed to me, Travis. You wanted to build a life with me, all while sleeping with someone else."*

*He reached for me, but I stepped back.*

*"Don't." putting both hands in mid-air.*

*"Please," he said, getting on both knees, "Let's just talk about this. This doesn't have to be the end. You don't want to live in this big condo alone, do you? Who's going to warm your feet at night? Who's going to be here to hear about your day?"*

*"I'll buy a fish, as my stomach dropped. At least it won't cheat."*

*Travis got on his knees and placed his arms around my knees, and began to talk into my thighs. "I made a mistake, and I am sorry."*

*"No, you made hundreds of them," pushing him away, "every time you lied. Every time you touched her. Every time you looked me in the eyes and pretended you loved me. I think your shit is worth more than your sorry."*

*He stood up. Frozen, not knowing what to say.*

*I walked to the door and yanked it open. "Get out."*

*"Bianca—"*

*"Out. Or I call the police," as I stared at the wall with a finger pointing to the hallway.*

*He hesitated, then turned slowly toward the door.*

*"Wait."*

*Travis looked back hopefully.*

*"You forgot my keys, this is MY condo," as I held my hand.*

*Travis hesitated in the doorway, his hand still resting on the frame as my furious eyes bore into him. He could see it, the heartbreak, the fury, the disbelief, and he tried one last time to reach me before it was too late.*

*"Okay," voice low, trembling, "I'm going to leave... but just one more thing. If I could take it all back, I would. I swear to God."*
*I folded my arms, my stare unflinching.*

*"Her three years," he continued, voice cracking, "could never amount to my love for you. You mean everything to me, Bianca. Everything. Don't throw away four years of us over this. Please...We reconnected for a reason."*

*I said nothing, so he took a step closer, his voice rising.*

*"She made me do it!" he blurted, "I swear she did. She was always stopping by when you weren't here. She came on to me! I was weak, I made a mistake, but it wasn't like I wanted to hurt you."*

*I blinked, then spoke slowly, each word like a dagger, "So... you had sex with her? In my house? In my bed?"*

*Travis didn't move.*

*"In. My. House?" I repeated, louder this time, my voice shaking with barely controlled rage.*

*"Bianca, please—"*

*"You have one second to get out of my sight before I do something I may or may not regret."*

*He moved then, realizing he had already lost me, but still trying to hold onto something that had long slipped through his fingers.*

*"Baby, I'm sorry," he said one last time.*

But the words fell to the floor, meaningless now. I turned away, fists clenched at my sides, doing everything I could to keep myself from breaking.

Travis gave me the keys, and I threw them across the room.

Travis had always been the kind of man who could charm a room without trying. He had a quiet confidence, a smooth voice that landed somewhere between comforting and seductive, and a smile that suggested secrets—some worth knowing, others better left alone. To me, he had seemed like stability wrapped in tenderness. A man who opened doors, remembered my class schedule, and brought me flowers for no reason. He wasn't flashy, not the loudest in the room, but he made me feel like I was the only person that mattered. He smelled good, he was tall, had dark brown smooth skin with hazel eyes, and the sex was undeniably the best I had ever had! The biggest penis I had ever seen too. For a long time, I believed he was my calm in the storm. However, there was another side of Travis that I eventually learned about. One that I probably overlooked because I didn't know what heartbreak looked like until it happened.

The moment the door clicked shut, my strength crumbled. I slid to the floor, my shoulders shaking with the sobs I held back. I thought about the love I had given so freely, the betrayal that had replaced it, and the friendship that had died with it.

Then, rising to my feet, I walked into the bedroom and opened Travis's closet.

One by one, I took out his clothes and began to slice them down the middle with a pair of scissors: shirts, pants, hoodies, everything. My hands trembled, but my focus never wavered. It was my version of justice.

*"You had the nerve,"* I shouted, tears streaking my face.

*"The absolute nerve to break me. TO BREAK ME."*

*My voice rose as I worked, words torn between heartbreak and rage. "You cheated on me... with her. With Tia. After everything I did for you. After everything I gave up for us. Why me, Travis? Why me!"*

My hands fell to my sides, the scissors dropping to the floor with a clatter. I collapsed onto the bed, curling into myself, the pain overwhelming.

In the quiet aftermath, I whispered one last plea into the dark.

*"God... what did I do to deserve this?"*

# Chapter 10: THE MAKE-UP

The following 2 months arrived with no mercy.

The October sunlight pouring through my windows felt almost cruel. I hadn't slept. My body had given up hours ago, but my mind hadn't let me rest. Images of Travis, of Tia, of everything I tried to build over the last four years, looped endlessly in my head like a film reel that wouldn't stop rewinding.

I had been praying and fasting for weeks, desperately trying to quiet the ache that lived like a pit in my stomach. It had settled there the day I learned the truth about Travis, Tia, and the betrayal that cracked my world in half. I prayed not just for clarity but for peace, for release, and for the strength to let go of the hurt that replayed in my mind like a broken record.

I wasn't trying to erase what happened. I just wanted to *breathe again*.

Every time I closed my eyes, I heard the echo of my own

words—sharp, cold, final: **"You two are dead to me."**

It haunted me. Because no matter how much I tried to believe I meant it, deep down, I knew I didn't. If something had really happened to them, if one of them had died without making things right, I knew I would never forgive myself. I would carry that guilt forever, stitched into my spirit like a scar.

As far as Travis, it took me weeks to finally realize that everything began to unravel during our junior year of college. It started small, missed classes, less energy, fewer texts returned. He stopped talking about internships and LSAT prep, started dodging questions with phrases like, "I'm just trying to make it through this semester." Then came the news that cracked everything open, he lost his academic scholarship.

I found out after noticing he wasn't registered for any spring classes. When I asked, Travis shrugged it off like it didn't matter. Said school was overrated. That the system was broken. That "working a regular job" might not be so bad. But behind his defiance, I saw something else: a deep shame he didn't know how to voice.

He never talked about it in detail, only vaguely referencing "things going on at home." I knew he had family issues beneath the surface, but he never let me in. He carried the weight alone and, instead of processing it, he let it bury him.

After that, he just went through the motions. Wake up, go to work, come home. No drive. No plan. No fire. I tried to hold him up. I told myself it was just a rough patch. That the ambitious, focused man I fell in love with was still in there, just buried under pressure. I encouraged him, prayed for him, sent him job listings, and helped him reapply for aid. But nothing worked. Travis had stopped chasing his dreams, and eventually, he stopped chasing us.

I realized I stayed longer than I should have because I was in love with the version of him that no longer existed. Part of me still hoped that version would come back.

I knew Travis had potential, not just the kind you see on paper, but the kind that you feel in your gut when someone talks about their future with fire in their eyes. I told myself that if I could just hold on a little longer, ignore the change, and push through the exhaustion of juggling school, emotions, and his growing indifference, things would eventually get better. Graduation was just around the corner. Then came marriage. And after that, I believed, hoped that life would settle into something beautiful, something familiar, something worth all the struggle.

After all, my parents had made it work. My father came home every night tired and grease-stained, and my mother never stopped moving, but their love never looked like a burden. They still danced in the kitchen. They laughed like teenagers. They chose each other every day. That was the love I had grown up watching, and somewhere deep in her heart, I believed marriage could fix what dating had broken.

Maybe once we stood before a church full of people, exchanged vows, and became "forever," that spark would reignite. Perhaps the ring would remind him of who he used to be and who he still could be. Maybe commitment would anchor him. Maybe love could really be enough. I was holding on to *maybe*. Not because I was naïve and avoided real problems, but because I believed in people. In building something, even after the walls had cracked. And more than anything, I didn't want to admit to myself or the world that the dream I'd invested so much in might already be over.

So, I smiled. I planned. I prayed. I waited for the man I loved to become the man I *needed*.

But now I'm done with Travis. That door is closed. But Tia and Stephanie? They were my sisters, my soul circle. We had shared childhood secrets, teenage dreams, and growing pains. They knew me in ways no one else did. And while my pain ran deep, so did my love. My heart had always been a self-sacrificing one. Even when I was hurting, I found myself thinking less about how I had been wronged and more about how to make it right. It wasn't weakness, it was my way of surviving and protecting what mattered most to me.

So, I kept fasting and praying, not for revenge or justice but for forgiveness, for the courage to open a door I had slammed shut, for the humility to say, *"I miss you,"* even when it still hurts, and for the hope that somehow, someday, we could find our way back to each other.

Because no matter how messy it got, I knew one thing for sure: You don't cut family out. You fight for them even when they break your heart.

One morning, I sat at the kitchen table now, silent, a half-drunk cup of coffee cooling between my fingers. My phone buzzed again. I picked it up without looking.

*"Hello?"*

*"Bianca?" came Stephanie's voice, hesitant and unsure.*

*I didn't respond right away.*

*"Yes? How may I help you?"*

*"I've been calling you for weeks. I even stopped by a few times, but you didn't answer."*

*"Okay?"*

*Stephanie sighed on the other end. "Look... I'm really, really sorry. I was in a bad position. I didn't know what to do."*

*"So, I guess you just took her side," I said sharply.*

*"It's not about taking sides, it was about staying out of it. I didn't want to lose either of you."*

*My voice softened, though my words were still edged. "I thought you were better than that, Stephanie. Some things are better left unsaid, but not everything."*

*"I know. I know, but I love you both. I was—*

*I exhaled deeply. "Look, I've been praying about it a lot. And I realized how vital friendships are. Nothing, nothing, should come between us, especially not a guy. Our bond has to be stronger than that. I love you. From now on, we will hold nothing back. Our communication has to get better, Stephanie. It has to."*

*There was a pause. Then Stephanie's voice broke slightly.*
*"Bianca, I promise. This was an eye-opener for me. It made me*
*realize just how much I love you, and Tia, too. I wouldn't trade*
*either of you for anything. God said in Proverbs 18:24, 'A man*
*of many companions may come to ruin, but there is a friend who*
*sticks closer than a brother.' And B... I'm that friend."*

*I smiled through watery eyes. "You're right. I'm sorry for how*
*I took it out on you. I didn't understand the position you were*
*in... but I'm not going to take all the blame either."*

*"I concur, I don't want you to take all the blame. It wasn't your*
*fault. Let's put this behind us, learn from it, and movveee on!"*

*I chuckled, "Have you talked to Tia?"*

*"Yeah... about five days after everything happened, in August.*
*But she hung up on me. She was still upset. I stopped by her*
*place too... but she wasn't there."*

*I thought for a moment. "I tell you what, we can drive over to*
*her place together. We need to resolve this. Life's too short."*

*"Okay, cool. Once again, B, I'm sorry for everything. I*
*should've just been upfront with you. I run my mouth about*
*everything else, I don't know why I didn't just say something."*

*"Stephanie," I said gently, "I already talked to God. I forgive you. You're like a sister to me. And I'd die if anything happened to either of you before we had the chance to make up. Now come on. I'll be outside when you get here."*

*"Wait... I have to drive all the way over there?" Stephanie whined playfully.*

*"Yes, heffa," as I laughed hysterically, "You're still in the dog house! You better be doing any and everything to make it up to me!"*

*"You're right. Let's do dinner too, my treat."*

*"Now you're talking," I said with a grin. "Bye, girl."*

I hung up and stared at the phone, heart lighter than it had been in months.

The healing had begun. I set the phone down gently, as though it were something sacred. My fingers lingered on it, my heart still catching up to the moment. The words still echoed in my mind, not just Stephanie's apology, but the Scripture, the promise, and the love in her voice.

A friend who sticks closer than a brother.

I wiped at the corner of my eye, where the tear had fallen so quietly, I hadn't even noticed. My heart had been hardened for months, choked by betrayal, drenched in sorrow. But now... something was loosening.

Forgiveness.

Not the kind that came easily. Not the kind that erased pain overnight. But the type that began with a choice, a choice to let go, to believe that love was still possible between people who had hurt each other.

I rose from the table and walked to the window. Outside, the sun was beginning to dip lower in the sky, casting warm gold across the tops of buildings. The kind of light made everything look softer, as though even the world understood she needed a new lens.

I took a breath. A real one. Not the shallow kind I'd been surviving on. This one reached my chest. I turned to the mirror and looked at myself. The woman who stared back was tired, yes, but different now. A little wiser. A little softer. Still cracked... but not broken. And for the first time in what felt like forever, I whispered aloud, *"God... thank You."*

I thought about all the nights I prayed for peace, clarity, and healing. And maybe healing didn't come like magic or thunder. Perhaps it came in awkward phone calls, tearful apologies, and tiny steps toward each other. Maybe it came in opening the door again.

When Stephanie pulled up and stepped out of her car, I was already there, leaning against the porch railing with a half-smile and arms wide open.

Stephanie didn't even make it up the steps before we embraced.

No words were needed, just the tight squeeze of two souls saying, I missed you. I forgive you. I'm still here.

We were filled with joy and nervous energy at the thought of finally reconnecting with Tia, so that everything else seemed to blur around the edges. In their rush to leave my condo, I forgot to use the bathroom, something I almost never forget. But none of that mattered. We had a mission now. After everything, the betrayal, the silence, the grief, we finally got a chance to show up for our sister. The bond that had once felt broken beyond repair had begun to mend, and the only thing that mattered was getting to Tia. To look her in the eyes, to say what needed to be said, and to remind her that she was never as alone as she thought. We weren't just visiting. We were making amends.

"That was really courageous of you to come to this self-realization, Bianca." As she continued to write down notes on her legal pad. She was already on the 4$^{th}$ page of notes by the time I took a breath to stop talking.

"Yeah, well, that wasn't the only thing I realized."

## Chapter 11: THE BREAKUP

I will never forget that I walked slowly toward Tia's apartment building, each step heavier than the last. The sidewalk under my feet felt unfamiliar, though I had walked it countless times before. My body moved on instinct, but my mind wrestled with a storm of thoughts that threatened to drown me before I even reached the door.

My heart was a mess. There was no neat word for what I felt. Anger, yes, betrayal, of course, but there was something deeper. Grief, that didn't quite belong to the loss of a boyfriend or even the collapse of trust. It was the grief of losing *history*, of watching the house of friendship I helped build from childhood burn to the ground, lit by hands I once held.

I had prayed about this moment and tried to rehearse what I would say. But standing this close to Tia's apartment again, the words didn't matter anymore. They didn't live up to the weight in my chest.

"What do you even say to someone who stabbed you while

hugging you?" I said internally.

As the building came into view, I felt my throat tighten. I remembered our sleepovers on my room floor, the whispered secrets under blankets, the nights we cried about boys and broken homes. We had grown together, survived together, and shared dreams of getting out, getting better, and finding a safer place.

And now here I was, standing on the threshold of Tia's door, carrying the weight of every lie, every choice, every unspoken betrayal.

*Was it worth it, Tia?* I thought. *Was he worth what we had?*

Stephanie walked beside me in silence, trying to match my stride, but she was falling behind. I could tell she was gaining weight. Stephanie was always plus-sized, but maybe the weight of this friendship caused her to eat more.

She said she had rehearsed this walk in her head a hundred times, what she would say, how she would stand between them, literally and emotionally, trying to hold together something that already felt shattered. But now, standing at the door, all her words disappeared.

She had always been the middle piece, the neutral one—the one who made peace and patched wounds with soft words a scripture and a smile. But this time, the wounds were too deep, too personal. And Stephanie had blood on her hands, too, maybe not from betrayal but from silence.

"I should've said something sooner, she said, I should've been braver."

I could tell the guilt weighed on her. She had watched it all unravel in slow motion, frozen between loyalty and cowardice. She told herself she was "staying out of it," but deep down, she knew the truth. She had stayed quiet because she was afraid. Afraid of losing us both. Afraid of being blamed.

She glanced at me. My expression was unreadable, but Stephanie could feel the tension radiating off me. She didn't know if I was walking toward forgiveness or one final explosion, and the uncertainty made Stephanie clumsy, tripping over her feet.

As I watched her regain her balance, I could tell she was thinking about Tia. She said she felt like she was walking into a battlefield with no armor. Just a heart torn in two and a prayer clutched tightly between her ribs.

*"God, please,"* she whispered, "Let this be the start of healing. Not the end of everything."

She told me several times that she didn't want to choose sides. She just wanted to help us remember what we meant to each other before everything got so messy, before boys, secrets, and pride turned them into strangers. Stephanie had always believed in reconciliation, in grace. But now, she wasn't sure if either of those things was still within reach.

My hand trembled slightly. My heartbeat was faster not just from anger, but from heartbreak. I wasn't just confronting someone who betrayed me. I was confronting the absence of the person I once loved like family. The person who had become a stranger.

I inhaled sharply and said to myself, *"I'm not here for revenge, I reminded myself. I'm here for closure. For clarity. For me.* As my hands began to clam. Still, I knocked. Because some truths, no matter how painful, had to be faced head-on.

*"I hope she's here."*

*"She should be,"* Stephanie replied, *"it's Tuesday. She only had that 8:00 a.m. class, and she works later tonight. She should be home."*

"We'll see," I said under my breath, knocked on the door, and looked through the blinds of her apartment window. I saw Tia.

She sat on the edge of the couch, blue jeans hugging her figure, and a laced bra. Fingers gripped the hem of her blanket, and she stared at the TV, but it didn't appear to be on. The apartment was quiet. She looked toward the door, already knowing without question who it was.

Her sisters, once. Her soulmates. The girls who had become her safe place when home wasn't one. The ones who walked beside her when her world was collapsing and never asked her to explain.

Now, she was the reason their worlds had fractured.

Tia leaned back, closing her eyes.

She heard the knock at the door. Her body stiffened, then rose slowly, each step toward the door. By the time she opened it and saw our faces, the words in her head had already turned defensive.

"What?" she snapped, the bite in her tone meant to shield the trembling in her voice.

*We looked back at her and then at each other to see who would speak first.*

*Stephanie took a slow breath. "Tia, we came to talk. It's been 2 months. We need to work this out."*

*"If y'all came to double-team me, you can forget it," Tia muttered, folding her arms.*

*I stepped forward. "Tia, I didn't come to argue or gang up on you. I just want us to work this out. Like three adults. Like best friends should."*

*"Now?" Tia raised an eyebrow.*

*Bianca tilted her head. "Ummm, I mean... unless you had a better time in mind, thennnn..."*

*"Well, yeah," rubbing her forehead, "I had class this morning and barely got any sleep last night. Come back around 2:30 once I'm showered and rested and not running on fumes."*

*Stephanie nodded. "Alright. But please, Tia, don't forget."*

*"I won't,"*

*"Okay?"*

*Stephanie smiled gently, "Tia?"*

*"Yeah?"*

*"Love you."*

*Tia paused, just for a second. Then, quietly closed the door.*

*Stephanie and I turned to leave, walking down the hall in silence until I suddenly stopped. "I gotta use the bathroom."*

*Stephanie smacked her lips. "Can't you wait? Let's just go grab dinner. I'm starving. You can go then."*

*Already turning back, "Girl, I'm not about to hold my bladder just because you're hungry. You're asking me to get a UTI!"*

*I walked back to the apartment, knocked lightly, no answer.*

*I knocked again, firmer this time.*

*The door opened.*

*Travis stood in the doorway.*

I became paralyzed. My stomach twisted. I thought I was sick. Every step I took toward forgiveness, every prayer I whispered for clarity, was shattered.

My body felt hot, like betrayal was burning through my bloodstream. But beneath the heat was something else, a drop, heavy and sudden. This was different. Deeper. My chest tightened as my vision swam. *Not her. Anyone but her.* I was prepared to forgive Tia for the past. But to see it-to witness the betrayal with my own eyes, in my presence, ripped the breath from my lungs. And still… somewhere in the chaos of my mind, I searched for a reason. A lie. A misunderstanding. Anything.

But there was nothing. Just the sight of my man, shirtless, in my best friend's apartment. My best friend. My sister.

Tia clearly didn't expect us to return to the door so soon. The moment she saw us, as she turned the corner from the restroom, her pupils dilated, and her arms were paralyzed. The damage was done.

Everything Tia had tried to hide, all the secrets she'd tucked behind excuses and delayed conversations, now stood in full view. And me, her best friend, was staring directly at the truth yet again.

"I don't know if I can continue to relive this. This is too much!" I said to the therapist.

"You are doing a great job. The only out is through."

I took a deep breath and rubbed my clammy hands together.

*Tia walked to the door behind Travis, "Why are you back here? I told you to come at 2:30."*

My face was red as blood raced through my body. *"You knew. You knew exactly what you were doing. You knew he was here. You dirty—"*

*I lunged, fury taking over, but Travis stepped between us.*

*"I know I shouldn't have trusted you! YOU DIRTY DOG! Why me? Your best friend since the fourth grade? Your sister! I was there for you when no one else was! And THIS is how you repay me?"*

*Travis looked down, his voice barely audible. "Baby, I had nowhere to go."*

*"Shut up, you piece of shit!" I snapped.*

*Tia stepped forward, pushing Travis behind her. "Don't talk to him like that in my house."*

*I stared at her up and down, "I cannot believe I was actually about to forgive you."*

"Forgive me?" Tia laughed bitterly, "What did I even do wrong? Took your man? Please. He left you. I didn't steal anything. He came to me because he wasn't happy. And it just so happened that I made him happy."

The words landed like slaps.

Stephanie entered just then, breath catching, "Tia, you're wrong."

"Oh, shut up!" Tia spat, turning on her, "You were just as wrong as me! Some friend you were."

"But I owned it," tears brimming. "We prayed about it. I was honest. I apologized. That's what friends do, they don't backstab each other, on purpose."

"Well, not all of us are as holy as you are, Stephanie!"

Stephanie shook her head, "You're going to regret this."

"I don't understand the problem," crossing her arms, "you couldn't keep your man. And now you're mad at me? Get out. Before I call the police."

*I turned to Stephanie, voice raw, "Let's go. I don't have anything else to say. And I sure as hell don't want to go to jail tonight."*

*But my words didn't stop there. I faced Tia one last time.*

*"I cannot believe you. And you have no remorse. Do you even feel anything? Everything that happened in your past, I protected you. I helped your brother and sister when nobody else would. When you didn't have money for college, who helped you? When you had nowhere to go, who took you in? Look around this room. Did Travis ever raise his hand one time?"*

*Tia looked down, then up again, "Look, Bianca... all I can say is I'm sorry. But for the first time in my life... I'm happy."*

*My voice dropped to a whisper. "With my man? WITH MY MAN?"*

*Tia's eyes narrowed as I asked. "How do you sleep at night?"*

*"The same way I did when everything in my life was taken from me. You just... learn to get over it. I appreciate everything you did for me. But I didn't know I had to pay you back."*

The room was so quiet it almost hummed with the weight of everything unspoken. No yelling. No tears. Just a thick, suffocating stillness that said more than anyone could find the courage to say. My eyes lingered on Tia for a single, burning second, not with anger, but something colder: finality. My face didn't twist. My fists didn't clench. I just stared. Then, without another word, I turned and walked out the door. And this time, I didn't look back. They were never who I thought they were. And maybe... just maybe... I didn't have to carry them anymore.

Stephanie followed a few steps behind. She was in a state of shock the entire time. She'd said she assumed, *hoped*, that Travis would have moved out after everything that happened. That he'd be gone like the mistake he was. But he wasn't. He was still there. Still in the apartment. Still with Tia. Still *Travis*.

And as much as she hated what he had done, what he had ruined, there was a flicker in Stephanie's body language that she didn't want to name. A twinge. A twist. Not Just anger. A look of confusion.

But it wasn't just that. When his eyes met hers across the room for a split second, she looked as if she saw something familiar. Something that hadn't quite died. Something dangerous. She quickly looked away, I noticed but was so angry I didn't acknowledge it. But Stephanie lagged just slightly behind, her silence no longer just about shock... but about something she couldn't yet admit.

# Chapter 12: CRACKS

After they left, I ran past Travis and entered the bathroom and closed the door behind me, the weight of my emotions pressing against my chest. Leaning over the sink, I reached for the roll of toilet paper, anything to dry the flood quietly. I wiped my eyes quickly, almost angrily, as if I could rub away the truth behind the tears. There were tears of guilt because of what I had done. Both feelings tangled inside me, warm and sharp, and neither one was easy to face. But they were honest. In that moment, honesty felt like the first step toward healing.

I wanted to tell myself that I didn't care, that I owed no one an apology, that if Bianca had really loved Travis, she would've kept him, and that if Stephanie had been a better friend, she wouldn't have let things spiral this far.

But the truth? The truth was that I didn't feel like I deserved good things. Not really.

I had spent my whole life building walls out of trauma and

calling it survival. And when Travis came around, charming and attentive, I let him inside those walls. Not because I loved him the way Bianca did, but because he made me feel seen, desired, and important, just for a moment. And I clung to that feeling like oxygen. But now, those moments were gone, and all that was left was the rubble.

I wanted to ask them why they had waited so long. Why hadn't they come sooner? Why did it have to be like this?

But I already knew the answers.

Because I was the one who had set the match, and now they were all standing in the ashes. Still, a small part of me, the girl who used to braid Bianca's hair, who used to cry in Stephanie's arms during nightmares, wanted something else.

Not forgiveness. Not even understanding. Just the chance to say, *I didn't mean to lose you*. But I didn't say it because I didn't know how to speak love without choking on fear.

***

I closed the book and immediately began to cry again. This is too much. I really want to leave." Putting my hands over my face, hiding my tears. "I just can't. I can't do this!"

"It looks like you have experienced quite a lot throughout your life, Bianca. We talked about this getting heavy. You are doing great. We have a lot to unpack here as I learn more about you. How about this, let's switch gears." Handing me Kleenex, when you are ready, let's discuss Travis. Have you spoken to Travis since college?"

Blowing my nose, gazing at the window, "it's funny you ask that, I ran into him last year. Partly why I am here. We had a nice, long talk at a coffee shop. I was walking in as he was walking out." Taking a deep breath, our eyes locked in disbelief as he held the door open for me.

Initially, I rolled my eyes and turned the other way, but he called my name loud enough that the entire coffee shop turned their heads. He had asked for a couple of minutes of my time, seeing that everything we went through was seven years ago. He always had a way with his words."

"What did you two talk about?"

"What happened after we saw him at Tia's house, what he experienced emotionally, and what he went through as a child

, and how he felt." Looking down my fingers as I let out a low sigh, after the conversation, "I know I should have said I wanted nothing to do with him and I still don't today, but why did I feel a sudden rush go slowly through my body, like I was supposed to help him?"

"Tell me more about his point of view at Tia's house and his childhood that made you feel a sense of empathy. Is that how you would characterize the feeling?"

"Yes, I guess."

# Chapter 13: TRAVIS

***

The bathroom steamed with heat as I stood under the showerhead, eyes closed, letting the water beat down on my back. But no amount of heat could wash away the tension curled in my muscles or the thoughts crowding my mind.

I ran a hand through my wet hair and exhaled, annoyed not at myself, but at how complicated everything was becoming.

Tia's always asking questions, always needing reassurance and trying to fix me.

She had been sweet at first. Supportive. Loving. Loyal in a way I hadn't experienced in a long time. After Bianca kicked me out, Tia opened the door literally and figuratively and made me feel like a man again. And I needed that. I needed someone to need me, to see past my flaws, to believe in me even when he didn't believe in myself.

But now?

Now she was slipping. She asked too many questions. Watched

me too closely. Pressed too hard on truths I didn't want to say out loud. Her love now felt conditional, like it came with strings. Like she was waiting for me to mess up.

I hated that. I hated how quickly affection turned into interrogation. Still, I couldn't leave. Not yet. Not when I had no money, no job, no backup plan. Not when he had nowhere else to go.

And besides… Tia still loved me. I could see it in how she looked at me, even now, even with the suspicion in her voice. That kind of loyalty was hard to come by. I just wish she'd stop digging.

I turned off the water and stepped out, wiping steam from the mirror.

My reflection stared back at me, tired and unshaven. Not the same man Bianca fell in love with. Not even the man Tia took in. Just a version of myself stuck in a spiral, too proud to admit I needed help, too scared to face who I'd become.

"I'm not the bad guy," he whispered.

In my heart, I didn't think of myself as a bad person. I rationalized my betrayal like a math problem: Bianca had her future, her books, her endless schedules and plans. I was just the guy trying not to get left behind. I convinced myself that Tia filled a void, that it was temporary, that it wasn't serious even when it was. What I didn't realize, or didn't want to admit, was that by trying to have both women, I was slowly destroying them both. I had thought I was in control, but I wasn't.

When Bianca finally confronted me and said my name with a tone so hollow it made my skin crawl, something inside me cracked. Not because I felt guilty, I had buried that long ago. But because I knew I had finally lost the one person who made me feel like the kind of man I wanted to be.

My parents never cared about me or what I did. My mother died from cancer. I know she was sick, but why did she have to leave me here alone in this world at only ten years old? I had to move with my father after fourth grade. He was there physically, but he often dismissed me to hang out with the plethora of women he had coming in and out of the house.

He had a pretty good life, childless in a sense, but overall, women took care of him. That's all I wanted, to feel wanted. To feel connected to something or someone. But the more I thought about the loss of my mother, the more I aligned myself with my dad's patterns. Always keep one on the side; that's how you shield your feelings. So, I learned how to charm women, how to make them feel like they were the only one in the world that mattered. After seeing it for so long, it became a natural instinct. I loved it. I showed them my potential, and they showed me theirs, then they showed me their wounds. Vulnerabilities, they thought they could trust me with. But deep down, I never intended to stay long enough to heal any of them, just long enough to forget my own. After losing my father last year in a car accident, I decided to stop loving. I mean, why love them? They were only going to leave. Look at my parents. Look at Bianca.

*After the shower, I came out in a towel and sat on opposite ends of the worn-out couch. The TV flickered quietly in the background while I focused on my laptop, tapping away at a computer game like the world outside didn't exist.*

*"I'm still hungry," I mumbled, eyes glued to the screen.*

*Tia glanced at me. "Okay?"*

*I looked up and stuck my neck out. "Okay? So get up and fix me something to eat."*

*Tia sat upright, folding her arms. "Baby, when are you going to get up and find something to do with yourself?"*

*Leaning back into the cushions, "You know I'm going through a lot, you said you'd be there for me."*

*"I have been, but baby, it's been 2 months now."*

*"What? You backing out now?"*

*"No!" she said quickly, raising her hands, "you know I'd never do that to you. I'm just saying... maybe it's time you go back to work. Just something small. Just to get moving again."*

*"I've been fired for months, the computer tech said he didn't need me anymore. Which is fine, because I don't need him either."*

*Tia blinked. "What? Why did you lie to me about that?"*

*"I don't know. Look, stop questioning me!"*

*"Are you gonna cook or not? What time you gotta be at work?"*

*She checked the time. "Um... four."*

*"Okay then, I want some lasagna."*

94

*"Baby, I gotta be at work at four,"*

*I shrugged. "Okay! So get in there and start cooking."*

*Tia stared at me. "It's already ten after one. It won't be done in time."*

*"If you stop running your mouth, it can be ready."*

*My laptop began to buzz. Tia's eyes darted toward it.*

*"Who is that?" she asked.*

*I stared at her. "Tia, please, with all these questions."*

*She bit her lip as she began preparing dinner. "Okay, okay. I trust you. I know you love me."*

*I left the room to get my charger, leaving my laptop open on the coffee table, not out of clumsiness but because no matter what I knew Tia wasn't going to leave me.*

*As usual, Tia's curiosity battled with her instincts. But then the screen blinked. An instant message appeared, glowing like a siren. She leaned forward and read the text.*

*"What time is she leaving, and why aren't you responding?"*

*"Travis!" she called out, voice cracking. I reentered the room naked, with a towel draped over one shoulder as the remaining water dripped down my body. "Yeah?"*

*She looked me up and down, caught off guard for a split second, then regained her consciousness.*

*"What is this about?" she asked, pointing to the screen.*

*I looked for a second too long. "Some lady. About a job." Turning away from the computer as if it didn't matter.*

*"A job?" she repeated, incredulous, I'm not stupid, Travis."*

*"Okay, I lied. It's a girl who wants to be with me, but I don't want her. You happy now?"*

*Tia's voice trembled, "how did she get your contact information? And what does she mean, 'Is she gone yet?' What is she waiting for?"*

*"I told you who she was. That's that. Either drop it or I'm leaving."*

*Tia's panic returned, rising quickly. "Baby, please don't leave... please don't cheat on me." As she got on her knees and opened her mouth.*

*"Look," pulling away from her, "I gotta finish drying off, and stop going through my stuff, you won't get your feelings hurt."*

*She stared at me, stunned. "What? What do you mean by that?"*

*I ignored her question.*

*"How did she even get your info, Travis? Why is she contacting you? Does she have your number as she stood up?"*

*"You see I didn't respond, so why are you sweating me? You think I'm cheating on you? If you can't trust me, then maybe you should leave me."*

*"No! I do trust you," Tia said quickly, "It's just... females messaging you out of nowhere. It makes me wonder. How do they even know you?"*

*"If I was cheating, I wouldn't have left my computer sitting right here," slamming my hand onto the table, "I never go through your computer, do I? Because I trust my lady. And I expect the same in return."*

*Tia's upper body dropped. "You're right, I trust you. I won't bring it up again. I won't go through your stuff anymore."*

*"Thank you," wrapping the towel over me again and moving back on the couch. "That's all I ask for. A little space."*

*Her phone buzzed. She didn't check it. She buried her face in her hands as she stood by the pot of food for a brief moment.*

*Then Tia began to stir the sauce gently in the pot and layer the pasta in the pan, the scent of garlic and tomatoes filling the air. "I was thinking about Stacey and Stanley today. I used to cook for them just like this."*

*I never looked up from my laptop, "Oh yeah?"*

*"Yeah." Her voice dropped slightly, "They don't want anything to do with me now. Not after everything I did for them."*

*"Mmhmm."*

*"It still hurts sometimes," she added quietly. I try to reach out online, but they never respond. I know they're doing fine, at least, I hope they are."*

*She mumbled, "sometimes I wish I'd just left and let them stay in that house. God knows what would've happened. But I'm the bad guy, right?"*

*She walked over to me, masking her sorrow with routine. "Okay, baby, the food's in the oven, and I'm heading out to work. I have a few errands I want to run first."*

*She leaned down and kissed him gently on the cheek. I barely kissed her back. I was no longer interested.*

*"Okay. Love you too."*

*I noticed Tia out of my peripheral vision, standing in the doorway for a second longer, hoping I'd turn around and say something real just once.*

*I didn't. She left.*

## Chapter 14: CAN YOU TRUST FAMILY?

*"What did I tell you about messaging me if I didn't message you first? You don't listen. I'm trying to keep things simple for us, baby. You can't be acting crazy on me. Okay? Now come over here. I miss yo sexy face."*

*The message was sent with a chime.*

*** 

*The living room was dim again, and the once-quiet apartment now buzzed with me lying lazily on the couch, tangled in the sheets with Stacey, Tia's younger sister. Her laughter bounced off the walls like sirens in the night.*

*"Whew, Travis baby!" Stacey grinned, breathless, "That was even better than the first round. No wonder your little chick is in love with you."*

*Smirking, "Nah, that was all you, baby. You put in that work. That's why I want to be with you so bad. You're amazing in bed and public."*

*Stacey giggled, tossing a pillow at me. "Well, you need to hurry up and handle this situation because I'm tired of sharing all of this in HER apartment." Looking around with her upper lip scrunching.*

*"Baby," pulling her closer, "you're not sharing anything. You got all of me. I'm just... staying there."*

*Stacey raised an eyebrow. "Oh. Well—whatever."*

*"I want to be with you forever," as I kissed her forehead, "we're gonna be perfect together."*

*Her eyes lit up. "I can't wait. Maybe one day, I'll meet your family and your friends?"*

*"In due time, we'll get there."*

*We laid there in silence until Stacey stretched. "I gotta get going. Long drive back. And I've got a doctor's appointment later."*

*"You okay?" hugging her from behind.*

*She laughed, "Relax. I'm fine. I just like messing with you. We did sleep together the first night last month, remember?"*

*"You pregnant or something?" Letting her go to look at her face-to-face.*

*She laughed harder, "No! Just my annual check-up. Calm down, Daddy."*

*"You scared me. But hey, if you were pregnant, I'd be happy."*

*She leaned in to kiss me. "That day will come, honey."*

*"You better go before we end up on round three."*

*"Okay! Okay!" she said, getting dressed.*

*"Hand me my shoes, please."*

*Moments later, the door opened, and the temperature in the room dropped like a stone.*

*"TIA!" Stacey's voice thundered.*

*"TRAVIS! STACEY?!" Tia said, dropping her purse onto the floor with her mouth wide open.*

*All three of us froze.*

*"Umm… Tia. I didn't expect you home so early. Remember you were talking about Stacey?*

*Stacey, brushing invisible lint off her tight jeans with a smug*

*grin curling on her lips. She didn't flinch. Didn't back down.*
*With a sweet but venom-laced tone, she looked toward Tia.*

*"Hey sis," she said, her smile twisted with satisfaction.*

*Tia stood frozen in the doorway. Her eyes bounced between me*
*and Stacey, struggling to piece together the puzzle of betrayal*
*laid out right in front of her. Her mouth opened, but no words*
*came, just a faint gasp, like the air had been knocked clean out*
*of her chest.*

*"His... girlfriend?" she echoed, her voice barely more than a*
*whisper, shaking like her knees might give out beneath her.*

*"You little slut!" she screamed, voice rising from the pit of her*
*gut, raw with heartbreak. Her body lunged before her mind*
*could stop her, fury outweighing logic.*

*I jumped between them, arms spread wide, pushing Tia back.*
*"LOOK!" I shouted, my voice cutting through the chaos, "calm*
*down. CALM THE HELL DOWN!"*

*But Tia wasn't hearing me not really. Not anymore.*

"Travis... Stacey... MY SISTER?! MY BLOOD?!"

Stacey crossed her arms, "Well, I'm just upset I didn't know you'd be home so soon. I wasn't ready for you to meet US yet."

"You backstabbing hoe!" Tia screamed, "Get out! Get OUT of my house right now! I protected you! I loved you! I took care of you! And this is how you repay me?"

Stacey's face hardened. "You want the truth? If you hadn't kept me from our parents, maybe I'd have some love for you. But no, you always wanted to be with your little friends. You didn't care about me or Stanley. Bianca wanted us to live with her. Like something was wrong with our home. Nothing was wrong with our family!"

"WHAT?!" Tia gasped.

"You heard me," Stacey snapped, "you tried to run from your past. But you are your past. You'll always be part of our family."

Tia's voice shook with rage and heartbreak. "You don't know what went on. You were only five! You don't understand, Derrick did things. Things that no child should endure."

*Stacey's eyes narrowed. "He never did anything to me or Stanley. But he went to prison because of you. You lied. And now I can't see him for another ten years!"*

*Tia's mouth fell open. "You don't know what you're saying…"*

*"Oh, I know exactly what I'm saying. And I waited. I waited until I was eighteen, created a new Facebook account, and added your boyfriend as a friend. And look what happened. I took what you loved, like you took what I loved. Eye for an eye, sis."*

*Tia's voice trembled as she stood in the center of her living room, her entire body shaking.*

*"So you messed with my man… because I was doing what I had to do?" she whispered.*

*Stacey, standing, shrugged without remorse. "I had to do what I had to do." The casualness of her tone hit like a brick.*

*Tia turned to me, eyes wide, heart collapsing. "Travis… how could you do this to me? You know how I felt about you."*

*I didn't even flinch. "Don't act like you didn't know I wasn't faithful," I said coldly, crossing my arms. "Hell, I cheated with you. You really thought it wouldn't happen to you, too?"*

*Stacey walked over to him with a laugh, wrapping her arms around his waist. "But he'd never do something like that to me," she said, leaning in to kiss him. "Right, baby?"*

*"Right."*

*I turned back to Tia, my expression suddenly laced with disdain. "You know what? Go pack my stuff. I'm leaving. I can't keep putting my real girl through this."*

*"Real girl?" Tia repeated, barely breathing.*

*"And to think I was looking out for you," Travis continued, shaking his head, "What was I thinking? Stacey needs me. I need her. Go on out to the car, baby. I'll be out in a sec."*

*Stacey grabbed her bag and sauntered toward the door.*

*Tia's legs buckled slightly. "Baby, please," she pleaded, "don't leave me. I have nobody. You're all I have. Please... stay."*

*But I had already made up my mind.*

*"Stop with the pity story, you wouldn't be in this situation if you hadn't told on your daddy for doing you so-called wrong. You*

*broke up your own family. That's on you."*

*"Baby—" she whispered.*

*"Stop calling me that," I barked, "it's Travis! You always playing the victim and always making people feel bad for you because of what you did. You brought all this on yourself. You've been weak since we were kids.*

*I'm going where a real woman appreciates me. Stacey drives down here every weekend to see me. I'm not gonna let her keep doing that alone. I'll be back over the next few weeks to grab the rest of my stuff."*

*Tia's jaw dropped. "Stacey? You can't be serious. She's a freshman in college. Travis, you're twenty-two!"*

*I turned slowly, "So what? She's got a future. She's in school. She's got goals. You? You're just... sorry."*

*Her knees gave slightly, but she continued standing.*

*"I want to be your wife," she said, tears blinding her, "we can start over. Please... just don't leave me."*

*I let out a short, sharp laugh. "Wife you? Girl, you've lost your damn mind. You were just something to hold me down until I got on my feet."*

*She gasped. "Travis…"*

*"Pack my stuff. I'll come get it later."*

*"Travis… baby… please," she begged, her voice hoarse with desperation.*

*"There's nothing to work on," I snapped. "Bye, Tia."*

*And then, without a shred of remorse, I walked out the door. A tactic I saw my daddy do time and time again.*

*Then came the scream.*

*"TRAVIS! BABY PLEASE! TRAVIS!"*

*But the door never opened again.*

"So, you believe that Travis' past makes you feel like you should accept what he did to you?" As she looked at me.

"Sorta. I mean, his world was turned upside down. His mother passed away. He only did what he saw his dad do. Then his dad died."

I pushed my hair behind my ear and looked down at the floor.

"So, should you accept if I was 30 minutes late to all of our sessions because I grew up in a home where people didn't have a sense of punctuality? And the more I'm late, the longer it would take for you to return to work.

She had a minor point, but it's not the same. This was my life she was talking about, my career, not my love life.

"I don't know. I understand his actions, but I just hate the way he broke my friend."

"How do you know he broke her? Is it written in your journal?"

"It is," I whispered.

"Care to share?"

## Chapter 15: CRISIS MODE

I collapsed onto the floor, sobbing. My world had finally broken open. The door slammed. The echo rippled through the apartment like a gunshot, sealing a fate that I hadn't been ready to face. I didn't move. I couldn't. There in the silence, surrounded by the scent of burnt lasagna and betrayal, the room heavy with the absence of the man I had clung to like a lifeline. My fingers trembled at my sides. My breath caught in my chest.

Everything was still. Then everything shattered. I screamed. It wasn't a word. It wasn't even coherent. It was the kind of scream that didn't come from the throat, it came from the soul. I was sobbing so violently my entire body shook. "Why me?" I whispered over and over again, rocking myself back and forth.

"Why always me?" tears continued to flood my face. "WHY ME!"

The apartment spun. My heart felt like it was folding in on itself, collapsing under the weight of abandonment. Stacey. My own sister. The girl I raised. And Travis... the man I gave everything to. My time. My body. My. loyalty.

Gone. Just like that. I crawled toward the wall and sat there, slumped and silent, my head resting against the cool paint as tears soaked my cheeks. My thoughts raced, but none of them landed. Flashes of my past swirled with the present. Derrick's angry voice, the sound of my own younger cries, the sting of every slap and silence I endured.

And now here I was again. Alone. Unwanted. Unworthy.

"He was never going to stay. No one ever stays." I said to myself.

I stood up suddenly, staggering toward the bathroom. My reflection in the mirror was a stranger: red eyes, matted hair, a face swollen from crying. I touched my cheeks, as if confirming I was still real. That this wasn't some twisted dream. I opened the medicine cabinet and stared at the rows of pills I'd collected from old prescriptions: sleep aids, painkillers, and anti-anxiety bottles I never finished. For a moment, my hand hovered over one. Then two. Then three.

# Chapter 16: IS IT TOO LATE?

***

*The late-afternoon sun filtered into my bedroom, casting warm shadows on the desk cluttered with laptops, medical school textbooks, and half-empty coffee cups.*

*"We need to take our cap-and-gown pictures before Thanksgiving break next week." As I typed on my laptop, "I can't believe it's been a month since I heard from Tia. We used to talk every single day. But... I'm glad I tried to make amends. I can live with that."*

*Stephanie looked up, her fingers stilling on her phone. "Oh shoot, you're right. And the price goes up after the break. Isn't it like $250 or something? I definitely don't have that kind of money right now." She paused, "and yeah... sometimes you just can't fix what's broken."*

*I sighed and nodded slowly, "Yeah, I guess you're right. And yes, it's $250, $260... something outrageous. But I'm still doing it. These last four years have been everything. I'll pay for yours too if you want, you can pay me back later."*

*Stephanie smiled and shook her head gently. "I appreciate that, I can't ask my parents for anything else. They just helped me with rent last week. I'll figure it out. Hopefully sooner than later." She yawned, "I can't wait to be done with this job and start making some real money."*

"Stephanie worked at the small bookstore just off campus. It wasn't glamorous, and the pay barely covered her groceries, but her love for books made it feel more like a sanctuary than a job. Still, it wasn't enough to live on. Her parents had been helping her stay afloat throughout college, always wiring money when rent was due or when she needed a little extra to get through the month. But they'd made it clear: once she graduated and fulfilled her student teaching internship, she was on her own. Not because they didn't love her, but because they believed in teaching responsibility through reality.

"My situation, by contrast, was a little more stable. I worked in the science lab, a job that not only gave me valuable hands-on experience in my field but also kept me close to my professors and mentors. My full scholarship covered tuition and housing, so most of the money I made went straight into savings. I was practical and disciplined, always thinking ahead."

*"You always manage to work things out, Steph. Just keep thinking about your future. That's what keeps me grounded."*

*Stephanie leaned back in her chair, letting out a laugh. "Yeah, I know! I've just been daydreaming about those fourth graders I'll be teaching next fall. Well, not solely teaching but gaining experience. I told you I reconnected with Mrs. Jefferies from Paul Elementary, right?"*

*"Oh my goodness! No! How is she doing?"*

*"She is doing great. Right before we came back to school in August, I went to Paul, and she was actually there decorating her classroom, and she remembered all of us. She was so proud of us, and we talked for hours. By the end of our conversation, I had an internship and a mentor."*

*"That's good! Does she still wear those knee highs?"*

*"That was the first thing I looked for, and yup, she had them on," laughing hysterically.*

*"I just can't wait till graduation when she officially takes me under her wing." Gazing into the sky.*

*I sipped my coffee, "Girl, I've still got fifty more years of school left."*

*"Well, you chose to be a doctor," Stephanie teased, "you could've picked something with way less schooling."*

*"I don't care. Being a doctor is my calling. Even if it takes forever. My daddy always told me that hard work pays off. Now, with that said, I've got to get started on this paper."*

*"Oh yeah! I brought my laptop too. I've got something due soon. When is yours due?"*

*"Next week, but I want to knock it out early. You know how these professors love surprise assignments."*

*Stephanie smiled. "B, you know why I want to teach fourth grade so badly?"*

*"Honestly, no. I never thought about it."*

*"Because that's the year I met my sisters," she said softly. "That's the year I met you. Met Tia. That was the most important year of my life. I love you both to death. And God said, 'He that loveth not, knoweth not God, for God is love.'"*

"Here you go with those Bible quotes. But I love you too, girl. Don't you ever forget that."

"I'm just glad I got you back. You being mad at me... that was killing me."

"I don't want to talk about that situation anymore."

"Understood." Stephanie's phone vibrated, and she looked down. "Well! I just got my cap and gown money covered. A member at the church is paying for it, she's super excited for me to graduate. Let's go next Wednesday?"

"Dang, that was fast!" Bianca laughed. "I need connections like that."

Stephanie shrugged playfully. "Favor ain't fair. Now come on, we're off track. Let's get back to these papers."

"You're right."

Suddenly, the doorbell rang.

They both turned to the door.

I stood. "Who is it?" I said in a deep voice, attempting to scare off any intruders.

*No answer. She opened the door and froze.*

*"Travis?"*

*Stephanie sat up quickly.*

*My voice immediately deepened, "What do you want? I told you if you ever came back here, I'd call the police. Stephanie, give me the phone."*

*But Travis looked different, disheveled, anxious, eyes dark with something I couldn't quite place.*

*"You need to get to the hospital," he said quickly. "Tia tried to kill herself."*

*The room went still.*

*"I came by to grab my last few things," he continued, "she was on the floor. Bleeding. There was a knife next to her... I don't know what she did to herself, but she wasn't moving. I think I got there just in time. I called the police, but I left when they showed up. Told them I'd just arrived."*

*My heart dropped into my stomach. Like a stone cast into deep water, pulling everything else down with it. Heat flushed through my body and then quickly left, replaced by a cold numbness that crawled up my spine and spread across my skin.*

*"No," I whispered. I stumbled backward slightly, steadying myself on the doorframe.*

My vision blurred, not with tears at first, but with disbelief. I couldn't process it. Tia. My Tia. Loud, vibrant, complicated Tia. The girl who would argue with a professor, laugh until she cried at dumb movies, and call three times in a row just to vent. The friend she had grown up with, fought with, forgiven, and mourned, even while she was still alive. Tia had tried to end it all. And I hadn't known. I had been here, laughing about graduation photos, worrying about rent payments, and drinking cheap coffee while my best friend lay bleeding on the floor. A sob tore from my throat before I could stop it. I turned to Stephanie, who looked just as pale, just as broken.

*"She was alone," I whispered, "she thought we didn't care." The guilt hit me like a crashing wave. All the anger, all the silence, all the boundaries I thought I was setting in the name of healing suddenly felt like punishment. Like abandonment. And now, it might be too late to make it right. Tears welled in my eyes, burning hot. "I let her walk away..." I choked. "And she nearly didn't come back."*

*"She's in the hospital now," he said, "I haven't gone to see her. I just thought... You should know."*

*Stephanie covered her mouth with her hand, eyes wide with horror. She hadn't cried yet. She was stuck.*

*"Why didn't I check in more? Why didn't I push harder? I let too much time pass. I had been so focused on school, on making things right with you, on avoiding the drama... that I had left someone behind. Someone I love." Stephanie turned toward me, her voice cracking. "We have to go. Now." Her hands shook as she reached for her phone, fumbling to gather herself.*

She followed me out the door, her prayer echoed loudly, "God, please... let us still have time to make this right."

*"Oh," Travis added casually, "Stacey's got another doctor's appointment, they think it's twins."*

*Before either of us could speak, he turned and disappeared down the hallway.*

*"Stacey?" I whispered, "her sister?"*

*Stephanie grabbed my arm. "Oh my God... we have to go. Now." We ran.*

## Chapter 17: THE RACE TO FORGIVENESS

The hospital stood at the edge of the city, tucked between two silent streets, surrounded by spring trees and a cold gray sky that never quite brightened.

It's walls were sterile off-white, too clean, too still, and yet somehow heavy, as if they absorbed the sorrow of every patient who'd passed through. The smell hit first: a mix of disinfectant, latex, and something faintly metallic like dried tears and blood too old to be remembered.

The mental health wing was tucked away on the sixth floor. It felt more isolated than the rest of the hospital, as if shame and suffering were meant to be hidden from the world. The lighting was soft but lifeless, too dim to feel safe, too bright to feel like rest.

Outside Room 617, time seemed to slow.

For me the hospital didn't feel like a place of healing. It felt like a confessional, a place where all our guilt, love, and unresolved words had followed us to sit in silence beside a friend who could no longer answer.

And as we stood outside that door, waiting to be let in, the walls around us didn't just smell of antiseptic. They smelled of fear, regret, and the fragile hope that it might not be too late.

*"I've been selfish all this time,"* I whispered, staring at the sterile white tile floor of the hospital hallway.

*Stephanie glanced over, clearing her throat, "What are you talking about?"*

*"I was only thinking about myself," I said, her voice cracking, "I got mad at her because of a man. After everything she's been through..." I choked on my words, tears beginning to well in my eyes.*

*"B..." Stephanie's voice softened. "What are you saying? You didn't do anything wrong."*

*I couldn't stop the tears now. "I should've seen it. I should've known. She was breaking, and I was too busy being hurt to see it."*

*Stephanie stood quietly for a moment, then offered, "Let me go check if we can see her."*

*I nodded, wiping my eyes. Stephanie stepped away.*

*She returned moments later. "They said she's not ready for visitors just yet, but we can wait out here."*

*I nodded again, my eyes distant, my heart wrecked.*

*Stephanie turned to me. "Now, please tell me what you meant earlier. What do you mean you were being selfish?"*

*I looked up at her, fresh tears streaming. "Because Tia never got the attention she needed from anyone. Not from her dad. Not from her mom. So, when the first man came along and gave her that attention, she clung to it. That's why she stayed with Travis. That's why she loved him even when he didn't love her back."*

*Stephanie shook her head. "Bianca, that's not your fault. None of that is your fault."*

*I was sobbing now.*

*"I got mad over something so petty and abandoned her too because I didn't want to deal with the pain. That's why she's here. That's why she tried to end it. Because she had no one left."*

"Tia, I'm sorry!" I cried into my hands.

Stephanie's own eyes welled with tears. She grabbed my hands.

"No, B. Stop. You are not to blame for what happened to her. You didn't hurt her. You helped her. You gave her a home, a safe place. You stood by her when no one else would. You've always been that friend."

My body shook as I tried to compose myself.

"She's going to be okay," Stephanie said gently. "The nurse said we'll get to see her soon. She'll remember that she's not alone when she sees us, her real friends."

"I love you, Stephanie," I whispered, "I don't think I can live without Tia."

"She's strong," Stephanie replied, "And so are you. Remember eighth grade? When we took your gym shoes and you had to walk barefoot all day?"

I let out a short laugh through her tears. "Yes... and I didn't talk to either of you for the rest of the day."

"That was the funniest day," Stephanie chuckled, "when she's better, we're having a sleepover, just like the old days."

*"And this time, with wine instead of Capri Suns,"* finally smiling. We sat in silence for a moment, hands clasped, waiting for the receptionist.

*A woman with kind eyes and a clipboard stepped up to us.*

*"Hi,"* she said gently. *"I'm the nurse. And you are?"*

*"Her sisters!"* I said, standing from the chair, staring into her eyes.

*"I'm glad to see someone came this time. Last month, she overdosed on pills and fell out outside as she was taking the garbage out. A neighbor found her. Once we pumped her she said she didn't have any family. So we didn't call anyone."*

*I practically lost my balance. "We had no idea!"*

*"Well, good thing you are here now. It's safe now to see her. She's stable, but she is in a lot of pain. We have her on a lot of pain medication, so right now, so be patient. Room 617, sixth door on the left."*

*"Thank you,"* they said in unison before rushing down the hallway.

*I was the first to burst into the room. When I reached the door, I shoved it open with both hands, as if hesitation would betray me one more time.*

*"TIA!" I cried, voice cracking as I stumbled into the room. The sterile light overhead stung her eyes, but nothing could have prepared me for what I saw. Tia looked so small. So still. Her skin was pale beneath the covers, her arms thin, tangled with wires. Her eyes were barely open. The sight struck me like a blow to the chest.*

*"Oh my God, Tia! Are you okay?" I gasped, running to the bedside.*

*Her body moved on instinct, her hands reaching out, her knees bending as she dropped to the floor beside her. Tears blurred her vision. Everything else, Stephanie's footsteps, the beep of machines, the antiseptic sting in the air vanished. All I could see was Tia. All I could feel was the fear clawing through my ribcage.*

*"Tia, say something!" I begged, "Please! Please talk to me!" Guilt flooded me, hot and sharp and choking. Every memory, every time I chose silence, every word I left unsaid rushed back like a tidal wave crashing through my chest.*

*"I'm sorry for everything," I sobbed, "I promise I am. Travis shouldn't have come between us. We've been through too much. Too much..."*

*I touched Tia's limp hands beneath her fingers, cold.*

*"I just want to say, I'm sorry for everything, and I just don't know how much longer I have," Tia said, gasping for air.*

*"We were supposed to grow old together," I whispered, "don't leave me now. Please don't leave me now." Tears were streaming down my face.*

*"I can't do this without you."*

*"Mail.. Mai.." Then Tia began to cough.*

*I jumped upright, "Tia? What do you mean by mail? What mail?"*

*But Tia's eyes fluttered, her breath rattled, and something shifted in the monitor behind them. That sharp, flat beep pierced the air. Her breath left her body.*

*"TIA!" she screamed. "Doctor! Nurse! PLEASE!"*

126

*And in the seconds that followed, as the medical team rushed in, I didn't feel like I was standing in a hospital. I felt like I was falling.*

*Falling into the realization that our apology had come too late.*

*"Ma'am, you have to leave," one ordered.*

*"No!" I screamed, sobbing uncontrollably, "TIA! I'm sorry! I'm sorry!"*

*Stephanie grabbed me, holding me back as the room swarmed with medical staff.*

*"It's okay, B," she whispered, tears streaming down her face. "It's okay."*

*But I broke free and burst back into the room.*

*"TIA!!!"*

*A doctor stepped in my path. "Ma'am, please. You can't be in here!"*

*"You didn't save my sister!" I yelled, trying to shove past him.*

*Stephanie rushed in, grabbing my arms. "Bianca, please! They tried! They tried everything!"*

*I collapsed into her arms, wailing, my voice hoarse, my body shaking.*

*"I'm sorry, Tia! I'm sorry! Please, Lord, bring her back. I need her! I didn't mean it, I didn't mean any of it! Please don't leave me, Tia. Please!"*

*The room went dim as the monitors fell silent. Outside, the hallway echoed with the sound of my grief and Stephanie's trembling whisper as she held me: "She knew you loved her, B. She knew. It's okay, B," she whispered through her tears. "It's okay… I've got you."*

"But it wasn't okay. Nothing about this was okay. Stephanie had always been the strong one. The faith-filled one. The one who believed that prayer could fix anything and that God never gave more than a person could handle. But now, as she held her best friend in her arms and stared at the unmoving body of the third member of their sisterhood, her faith felt fragile.

"She buried her face into my shoulder, trying to hold both of us together. Because if she didn't, we'd both fall apart."

## Chapter 18: THE BLACK OUT

"The last time I saw your dad, Pastor Richards, was at the funeral. I hadn't seen your family in so long!" said Ms. Jefferies.

"Yeah, I hadn't seen him in so long either. I changed churches before graduation." Looking into space.

"Speaking of Pastors, the funeral was a mess! Who planned that? I know we never talked about it, but did I miss something? Run it by me again!"

"Ms. Jefferies, you're asking me to open up all my wounds. I haven't heard anything about you."

"I will be happy to share, but as your mentor, I need to make sure I am there for you in the ways you need me more than the ways I need you. But my word is my bond, and I will be happy to share after we discuss this funeral. You can't leave me hanging like that!" as she chuckled and tapped my shoulder.

I gave her a half curve of a smile, "I really don't remember much... Everything blacked out for me."

---

## Chapter 19: AT THE ALTAR

"Due to the holidays, the funeral was held after the New Year on January 12th. This also gave Stephanie and me time to grieve and ensure the arrangements were perfect for our friend. The church was silent except for the low hum of the organ and the occasional sniffle echoing across the pews. Soft light spilled through the stained-glass windows, casting a rainbow of colors on the casket centered before the pulpit. The flowers around it were white and yellow.

"The pastor, Stephanie's father, stepped forward, his voice gentle but clear. *'Is there anyone who would like to share a few words about Sister Tia Davidson? You're welcome to do so now.'*

"From the left side of the room, I rose slowly. Each step I took toward the pulpit felt heavier than the last. I faced the congregation, my hands clammy, trembling slightly, and my eyes already brimming."

*"Thank you, Pastor," I began. "And thank you to everyone here who came out to celebrate the homegoing of my best friend."*

My voice wavered, but I pushed on.

*"I loved Tia. I still love her from the bottom of my heart. She wasn't just my friend, she was my sister in every way that mattered. Blood couldn't have made us closer."* A tear slid down my cheek, and I let it fall. *"She was strong. Stronger than anyone I knew. She carried burdens most people couldn't even imagine. And yet, she still made room to carry the people she loved."*

*I paused to gather myself.*

*"In four months, Tia was supposed to walk across that graduation stage with me and Stephanie. But now…"* I looked toward the casket. *"Now she's walking with us in spirit."*

Then I saw them, Travis and Stacey walking in right after Ms. Jefferies, slipping into the back of the room. My chest tightened.

*"But I believe that God makes no mistakes,"* my voice trembling, *"So I'm trusting that even in this, there is purpose. I just want you to know, Tia… I love you. And I'll never stop loving you. I'll be here for your family. I'll carry your memory forward because you carried all of us for so long."*

I stepped down, wiping my eyes. Stephanie stood and made her way to the pulpit. Her hands were clasped tightly, and her legs were buckling.

*"I want to echo what Bianca said, thank you, everyone, for being here,"* she said softly, *"Tia meant so much to us. She taught us how to fight, laugh through pain, and hold on to love even when life gave us every reason to let go."*

Suddenly, a voice cut through the silence.

*"Um... can I say something?" Travis asked, stepping toward the front.*

*Stephanie froze. My head snapped up. Travis didn't wait for permission. He walked straight to the pulpit and took the microphone.*

*"I just want to clear the air," he said, eyes scanning the room, "Tia didn't die because of me. She had a lot going on that y'all probably didn't know about. I was just another pea in the pot."*

*The crowd murmured in confusion and discomfort.*

*"What in God's name is going on?" Someone whispered from the pews.*

*Stephanie took a step forward. "Travis."*

*"Naw, naw," he cut her off, "don't 'Travis me'. I just want the truth out. Yeah, I broke up with her. But she made her own choices. I wasn't happy, so I left. And I'm not gonna stand up here and act like I feel bad when I don't." He gave a short, humorless laugh.*

*I stood, rage radiating off me like heat.*

*"Travis. Get. Out. NOW." But he raised his voice instead.*

*"And on that note, yeah, I'm gonna leave this funeral. Because my ex-fiancé, whom I still love, asked me to. Bianca, baby, I still love you! Kids or no kids, I'm here if you want me back!"*

*The room erupted in whispers and disbelief.*

*"I'm a good man, come on baby!" he called, grabbing Stacey's arm, "let's go. We're not wanted here."*

*But Stacey didn't move.*

*"No," she said, snatching her arm out of his hands, "you're not wanted here."*

*She stepped away from him, toward the pulpit. "This is my sister's funeral. And I was foolish enough to betray her. Now she's gone. And I can't undo it."*

*The room went silent again.*

*"I've gone to see my father in prison many times," Stacey continued, "and he never told me what really happened. Not until after my sister died."*

*Her voice cracked, "I believed him. I believed them. And now I can't have my sister back."*

*I moved to quiet her, but Stacey raised a hand.*

*"No. Let me finish. That's why these families are so dysfunctional. Everything's always a secret. Everything's always hush-hush. And now look where it got us, here. At her funeral." She gestured around the room, breathing hard.*

*"My mother isn't even here," she said bitterly. "She's too busy sending money to the same man who abused Tia for years. Tia raised me. She raised Stanley. She was more of a parent than our parents ever were. And she died carrying the weight of all our silence. Stanley is not even here. He doesn't even know the truth. He removed himself from this entire family!"*

*People in the pews began to cry.*

*"I was five or six. I didn't know. I didn't understand. But now I do. And I helped kill her too. I didn't know what I was doing, but I still did it. And I'll never be able to make it right."*

*The crowd stared at Stacey in awe as their pupils widened and their hands went over their mouths.*

*"I'm three months pregnant with his kids," she added. " I don't even want him. I just wanted to hurt my sister. And now I can't take it back."*

*She turned to me, eyes glistening. "Bianca.... Me and Travis, we're done. I don't want anything from him. I just want peace. I just want to stop pretending."*

*She turned back to the casket, "And I hope... I pray... that God can forgive me." She stepped down.*

*The silence in the church was deafening. Not one cough. Not one shuffle. Just the sound of hearts breaking and truths finally finding their way into the light.*

*"Done?" he scoffed from the side aisle, stepping back into view. His eyes locked onto Stacey like she still owed him something.*

*"You say you're done with me? You got my kids, baby."*

*Stacey stood tall, voice calm but deadly. "And that's all I got, yo kids." Gasps rose softly from the congregation, but Stacey didn't falter.*

*"Unfortunately, my children won't have the luxury of growing up with both parents. And that's not on me, that's on you. You're a sorry excuse for a man, Travis. I don't know how my sister or Bianca ever put up with you."*

*Travis's mouth opened, but no words came out. "I'm done with you," Stacey said firmly. "I'll let you know when the babies are born. Whether you choose to show up in their lives or not is on you. But for all I care? You can stay gone."*

*She turned sharply and walked down the center aisle, never once looking back. The echo of her heels was the only sound until she disappeared through the double doors.*

*I sat frozen near the aisle, my arms crossed tightly over my chest. My eyes didn't follow Stacey as she left, they stared blankly at the altar, like I was trying to hold myself together from the inside out.*

*Stephanie moved beside me slowly, cautiously, as if afraid she'd say the wrong thing again.*

*"What just happened?" Stephanie whispered.*

*I didn't answer right away. I began moving my hair out of my face.*

*"Everything," I finally said. "Everything happened. At once. In front of everybody."*

*Stephanie looked down at her shoes. "At least... now we know the truth."*

*My eyes snapped to her. "Do we? Because every time I think I've heard the last secret, another one crawls out of the walls."*

*Stephanie looked away. "You're right."*

*I shook my head, exhaling hard through my nose. "Tia's dead. And now Stacey wants to rewrite the past like it will fix something."*

*"She's grieving, B."*

*"We all are, but that doesn't erase what she did."*

*The church around them felt too quiet, too empty, like the silence after a storm. The kind that makes you wonder if the worst part has already passed or if it's just beginning.*

*Stephanie placed a hand gently on my arm. "You're not alone, you know."*

*I didn't move. But I didn't pull away either.*

*"I know," I said quietly. "That's the part that hurts the most."*

*Stephanie rose back to the pulpit as the congregation waited as if they were waiting for the next scene of a movie.*

*"I'd like to apologize to everyone here for the ignorance we've all just witnessed," she said, her tone cutting through the tension. "But don't worry, you won't have to deal with that again."*

*She paused, her breath catching.*

*"I want to say something about Tia," she continued, eyes shining with emotion. "She wasn't just my friend. She was my sister. A second mom in a lot of ways. She saw things in me I hadn't seen in myself. And she always showed up, even when no one else did."*

Her voice cracked. *"I'm really, really going to miss her."*

Stephanie stepped down without another word, the grief clinging to her shoulders like a wet coat. She returned to her seat and stared blankly ahead, hearing everything and nothing at once.

From the side aisle, Travis's voice broke through again.

"Stephanie, you ain't no saint either, so don't stand up there acting like you are." Heads turned. "But whatever," he added bitterly, "I'm outta this place. This reminds me too much of my mother's funeral service.

He stormed out, slamming the side door behind him. The final echo of his exit left a deep silence in its wake. The crowd remained stunned, murmurs rippling across the pews.

"Lord, have mercy," whispered a woman in the pew behind me, "That whole family's going to hell."

Another churchgoer gasped, "Not in God's house! Lord, forgive her!"

The pastor cleared his throat, stepping up slowly to the pulpit. His voice, though shaken, regained the rhythm of reverence. "We will... uh... have the burial at Sixth and Green *immediately following the service." He paused, looking out at the faces still flushed with confusion and emotion, "but first," he said firmly, "let us pray." He bowed his head.*

*As the prayer began, eyes closed across the room. Some bowed their heads in repentance. Others are in pain.*

*The sanctuary had nearly emptied after the Eulogy, and the last murmurs of the congregation faded beneath the hush of heavy footsteps and quiet tears.*

*I sat motionless as my eyes fixed on the closed casket as if I expected it to move, to open, to reverse time. Stephanie sat beside me, hands folded in her lap, lips pressed together, her body small beneath the weight of regret.*

*My parents walked up and sat on the other side of me.*

*"She would've hated all that drama," my voice barely louder than a breath.*

*Mom gave a soft, tearful laugh. "She would've laughed at it later. Called it 'a hot mess on holy ground.'"*

*A small smile pulled at the corner of my mouth, but it faded just as quickly. I let out a long breath and stared straight ahead. Daddy came to console me and told me everything was beautiful. I always loved how kind he spoke of things no matter how messy they got.*

*"I kept waiting for her to walk in late," I continued, "sit in the back, rolling her eyes, whispering under her breath that this was too much. But... it's real now."*

*Stephanie nodded slowly, her throat too tight for words. A silence fell between them, thick with things neither knew how to say.*

*"I keep thinking," Stephanie said finally, "if we just... did something earlier. If we'd called more. Prayed harder. Listened deeper... maybe—"*

*"I did everything I knew how to do," I said, cutting in gently. "She was carrying everybody else's pieces."*

*Stephanie lowered her head, a fresh wave of guilt building behind her eyes. She whispered, "I wish I had told her I loved her before it was too late."*

*"She knew." My voice cracked ever so slightly. "We all did, even when we were too proud or too hurt to say it out loud."*

*Stephanie wiped her cheek with the back of her hand. A tear slid down her face anyway. Mom and I reached over and placed our hands over hers, not in forgiveness, but in shared grief. We sat like that for a while. Saying nothing and breathing in the silence.*

*"We didn't save her," I said finally, "but we can carry her. From here on out."*

*Stephanie nodded, her eyes red and full, "Then let's carry her right."*

*I exhaled, like I had been holding my breath since the moment I got the call.*

*"No more secrets," I said.*

*I looked over at her. "And next time I ask who I can trust... I want to say your name without flinching. I want you to tell me everything, no more silence. Can I trust you?"*

*Stephanie didn't answer with words. She just lowered her head, humbled by the grace that hadn't been earned but was offered anyway. She just sat there, silent, the guilt pressing down on her so hard she could barely breathe.*

*Then I added, almost to myself but loud enough to be heard, "Trust can break... but so can silence." I nodded once, my gaze never leaving the casket.*

## Chapter 20: WHO CAN YOU TRUST

Spring had returned with a gentler sun and softer air. The campus had come alive again, trees budding with new leaves, students moving in clusters between classes and dorms. But the world still felt paused for me and Stephanie, gray in the corners where Tia's absence had settled.

*"I'm so glad we made it back to school after spring break,"* Stephanie said as they stood at the front of the crowd gathered in the courtyard. *"But I'm even more thankful they approved the memorial walk for Tia. It feels good to be doing something that truly matters. Praise God!"*

*I looked out at the sea of faces. There were classmates, neighbors, faculty members, and strangers all standing quietly in remembrance. My eyes softened with gratitude.*

*"Yeah,"* I whispered, *"Look at them. All these people here... for her. I wish I could thank each and every one of them. They didn't have to come."*

*"They didn't,"* but they did. Are you ready to start this?"*

*I nodded and stepped forward, raising my voice gently to the crowd.*

*"First, thank you all so much for coming out today to honor our dear friend, Tia Davidson. It means the world to Stephanie and me that so many of you have set aside your time to support this cause. Tia was more than a friend, she was light. And today, we walk to carry that light forward." Stephanie took over seamlessly.*

*"We'll be walking one mile from here to Tia's old apartment. When we get there, feel free to leave candles, balloons, stuffed animals, or anything you brought at the tree beside her building. Thank you again for being here. Let's begin."*

*The walk started in silence. Each step seemed to echo with memory. Stephanie rubbed her stomach subtly as they moved, a hint of discomfort crossing her face.*

*"You okay?" I whispered.*

*"Huh? Oh-yeah. I'm fine," Stephanie said, forcing a smile, "just thinking about Tia."*

*I studied her for a second, but let it go and continued to draft an email on my phone with every step I took. Twenty-five minutes later, we arrived. The tree outside Tia's apartment had become a quiet shrine. Balloons were tied gently to its trunk. Candles flickered in the breeze. Plush bears leaned against it's base, and handwritten letters fluttered in the wind like whispered prayers.*

*"Thank you all again," I said to the group, "for your prayers, love, and presence. I know Tia would be proud." The crowd clapped softly, then slowly began to disperse.*

*Inside the apartment, the air was thick with memory. The walls still smelled faintly of vanilla, her favorite scent. Folders, books, little trinkets from college life, everything remained, waiting to be sorted through by hands that knew her best.*

*"I'm so happy with how that turned out," Stephanie said.*

*"Yeah," I murmured, "Me too. It's just... everything has happened so fast. I am just glad we got through the arrangements and the memorial, and I had time to mourn her loss and process everything!"*

*Stephanie picked up a photo frame and ran her fingers across it. I gently folded clothes into boxes.*

*"What are we doing with all this stuff?" Stephanie asked, "I*

*don't have space for even half of it."*

*"I'll take most of it to my place, Stacey said we could let her know if we needed help. Oh, and I told her about graduation. She said she'll come to support, for Tia's sake," as I lifted a box and found a journal with my name on it. I immediately put it in my purse before Stephanie could see. I wanted to read it alone. Who knows what she wanted to share with me."*

*"That was really mature of her. What a blessing."*

*"Don't you have something you want to share___"*

*The doorbell rang.*

*I went to answer. "Probably Stacey." I opened the door and froze.*

*My presence didn't make a sound, but it hit like thunder. I blinked, unsure at first if it was real.*

*The woman's eyes were tired, her hands wringing the handle of a small purse like it was the only thing keeping her grounded. Her clothes were tidy, but her energy frayed. And behind her frail demeanor, I could still see the steel wall of avoidance and years of silence.*

"Mrs. Davidson?" I said, squinting. The older woman looked down, her hands clutching a small purse,

"Stacey dropped me off. I heard about the funeral... and I wanted to come to thank you both. For everything you did. You stepped in as family when I failed."

"No," I said firmly, "you didn't fail to be there. You chose not to be. And with all due respect, I don't want to hear excuses. You missed your daughter's funeral. No apology can cover that."

"I know, you're right. And I don't expect forgiveness. I just wanted to try. Tia... she deserved better. And without you two, she might not have made it as far as she did."

Stephanie stepped forward. "You're right. But Bianca and I have a lot to do, and we don't have time to sit here and make you feel better. You should've done that with your daughter when she was still alive."

"I'm not sure what I was thinking coming here," Mrs. Davidson whispered, "Stacey said it would help, but... maybe I was just afraid of losing all my children. I just found out that Derrick passed away right after the funeral. The warden called me... it was suicide. He left a note telling me to 'make it right since he couldn't.'"

"No," I snapped, "you aren't here to make it right because you care, and even if you were, Tia is no longer here! You knew what he did, and you stayed quiet. Now that he has finally admitted it and is dead, you want to play the victim."

Mrs. Davidson stepped back. "I see I'm not welcome here."

"You guessed right."

Without another word, she turned and left, disappearing down the hallway.

I slammed the door.

"I can't believe her, she only came here because the truth's out and her man is dead. She didn't care about Tia. She just didn't want to look bad. She is still under his spell even after her death. And if she thought she was getting any of Tia's things, she's delusional. I tell you, you can't trust anybody in this world nowadays! Everybody is always lying about something! Who can you trust? I can't trust anybody!"

"Bianca…" Stephanie's voice was soft.

"She probably wanted to dig through her stuff—" as I paced back and forth at rapid speed with my hands on my hips.

"Bianca."

"She is one of those people, you know? The ones who lie and manipulate and—"

"Bianca!" Stephanie yelled.

"What?!" I stopped in my tracks.

Stephanie's eyes welled. Her voice came out fast, like it had been locked in too long.

"A couple months ago…" Stephanie's voice trembled as she stared at the floor, unable to meet my eyes, "I went to Tia's house. I just… I wanted to see her. To talk to her. To make things right."

She paused, swallowing hard, her breath shaky. "But she wasn't there. Travis answered the door. He was picking up the rest of his things."

I stood utterly still, my arms slowly folding across her chest. A wall was forming, and Stephanie could feel it, brick by brick.

*"I told him everything,"* she continued, her voice growing quieter. *"I told him how I blamed him for everything, how our*

*friendship with Tia was unraveling. I was crying... I was hurt... I just—I didn't expect him to care. But he did. At least in that moment, it felt like he did."*

*She finally looked up, her eyes glistening.*

*"He comforted me. He said all the right things. He asked me to pray for him, and I did. He told me he regretted everything... that he didn't mean to hurt any of us. And I believed him. I forgave him."*

As she told the story, she flashed back on that day.

*When the door opened, he stood there, sleeves rolled up, a half-packed box on the floor behind him.*

*"Oh," he said, surprised. "Hey... Stephanie."*

*I hesitated. "Hey. Is Tia here?"*

*He shook his head. "Nah... she's not. Haven't seen her since earlier this morning. You okay?"*

*I wasn't okay. Not even close.*

*My throat tightened. "Can I... just come in for a minute?"*

*He stepped aside, and I walked in slowly. The apartment felt hollow, part memory, part regret. Cardboard boxes sat scattered near the walls, half-filled and forgotten. I stood there for a moment, unsure of why I'd even come.*

*"I know this is weird," breaking the silence. "I just... I wanted to talk to Tia. But since you're here..."*

*My voice cracked. I hadn't planned on crying, but my eyes were already burning. Everything I had bottled up the guilt, the distance, the memories of the three of us laughing in classrooms and staying up all night during finals week—was bubbling.*

*"She's not talking to me, and honestly, I don't blame her. I feel like I failed her. And you—" biting the inside of my cheek, "—you broke her."*

*Travis didn't argue. For once, he didn't try to defend himself.*

*"I know," he said, sitting down slowly. "I broke a lot of things."*

*I wiped at my eyes, laughing dryly. "I'm mad at you, Travis. But I'm also mad at myself. And I don't even know how we got here."*

*He motioned for me to sit, and I did, reluctantly. There was*

*space between us on the couch, but it wasn't much. "You've always been the strong one," he said softly. "The voice of reason. Tia and Bianca always looked to you. Hell, I did too."*

*I looked away. The compliment shouldn't have mattered, but it landed. I didn't feel strong. I felt worn out. Forgotten. Used up.*

*"I've been praying for her. For us, you too, honestly. As much as I didn't want to."*

*He looked at me then, directly, gently. "I don't deserve your prayers."*

*I shrugged. "None of us do. That's grace."*

*We both went silent for a minute.*

*Travis reached out, just slightly, his hand brushing against mine. "Thank you," he whispered.*

*The touch was small. Barely there. But, in that moment, it felt like oxygen.*

*I didn't move my hand.*

*"I'm sorry for everything," he said again. "I swear I didn't mean for it to get this far."*

*His voice was low, almost trembling. And the way he looked at me, broken, vulnerable, human, it reminded me of the version of him I used to believe in. Before the lies. Before the betrayal. Before it all fell apart.*

*One tear slipped from my cheek.*

*"I don't even know what I'm doing anymore," I whispered.*

*"Pray for me," he said softly, taking her hands into his own.*

*I closed my eyes and began to pray. Words flowed from my mouth, words of forgiveness, redemption, and reconciliation. I asked God to heal what had been broken and cover them in grace. But even as my lips moved, my mind told a different story.*

*I wasn't praying for Travis. I was praying for myself not to fall into the very temptation that now sat inches away, looking at me with eyes that no longer seemed dangerous, only broken. My hands trembled slightly in his. I told myself it was just emotion, just compassion. But deep down, I knew it was more than that. It was confusion wrapped in warmth. Guilt tangled in desire.*

*When the prayer ended, the room didn't move. Neither did we. Silence stretched around us like a net, pulling us closer without words. No one reached first. No one pulled the other in. But somehow, our bodies closed the space, the gravity of shared pain doing what logic could not stop. And that was all it took.*

*A shared wound. A shared silence. One fragile moment of weakness. One bad decision born from months of betrayal, broken trust, and blurred lines.*

*I wasn't thinking about Bianca. I wasn't thinking about Tia. I wasn't even thinking about myself, not the self I usually protected, the girl with a bright future and clear morals. That girl had gone quiet. I was thinking about all of the times I had conversations with my friends about their experience with Travis.*

*As our clothes slowly fell away, I noticed the scent of his cologne, the very one Bianca used to describe with dreamy eyes. This made me feel weak. I knew it was wrong, but it felt so right. He knew just how to touch my curvy body. His soft lips caressing my neck made me feel like I was the only woman in the world that mattered. I remembered the late-night phone calls with Tia, laughing as she blushed and shared private details of how Travis made her feel desired, worshipped, and wanted. I felt that. His manhood was just how Tia explained it.*

*I felt it now. Not in the way I thought I would, but enough to make me pause. Part of me wanted to stop. To back away, but another part was curious, aching to know what made both of my best friends fall so hard for this man. I was a virgin, untouched and guarded for so long. I had nothing to compare this moment to. Nothing but curiosity… and a craving to feel something different than shame, guilt, or regret. He slowly picked me up and made our way back onto the couch. He kissed me gently and promised to take his time with me so it could be special. He then whispered in my ear that he was glad I lost my virginity with him and not anyone else because he knew what my body needed. After all, we had known each other for so long.*

*I knew it was wrong. But at that moment, knowing wasn't enough. I just wanted to feel something real. Even if it meant falling into something fake, in the end, all I could remember was the moment after, the one where my breath caught in my throat, and I realized, this wasn't comforting. It was a collapse.*

My brow furrowed, my breath catching in my throat. I stood staring at her as she finished her story.

Her voice cracked as the words tumbled out.

*"One thing led to another. I didn't mean for it to happen. I didn't plan it. I was vulnerable and he, he took advantage of that moment. And I..."*

*She paused again, as if saying the next words might shatter what little was left of the air between them.*

*"...it happened. And now... I'm 6 months pregnant. With his baby."*

*Stephanie wiped at her eyes, her fingers trembling.*

*"I didn't tell you because I didn't want to lose you, too. I already lost Tia. And I know, know that this was wrong. I'm not asking for you to understand, but I needed you to hear it from me. I haven't told anyone. My parents will disown me if they find out, and I will be the talk of the church. I am so sorry, Bianca, I just don't know what to do. I have no money for an abortion, plus it's too late, and it goes against my religious beliefs."* Stephanie stood, her voice shaking, but trying to sound sincere. *"I'm so sorry, Bianca,"* she said quietly, *"I didn't know how to tell you. I didn't plan it. I just... I was broken."*

*I didn't speak. I didn't cry. I didn't blink. I just stared at Stephanie, like I was looking through her instead of at her.*

*"Do you remember when I told you I forgave you?"*

*Stephanie nodded cautiously.*

*"I don't." I said coldly.*

The silence snapped like a wire pulled too tight. I stood slowly, my movements unnervingly calm. I walked to my purse and pulled out a plain white envelope. It had no return address. I tossed it onto the table between us.

*Stephanie stared at it. "What is that?"*

*My voice was hollow, "it came in the mail a couple of weeks ago, right after Tia's passing." Tia's last words were "mail," but I had no idea what she meant until I got that letter. I've been carrying it around, waiting for the perfect moment."*

*Stephanie hesitated, then reached for the envelope. Her breath caught as she pulled out a photo of her and Travis, unmistakably close, in Tia's apartment. The timestamp in the corner said it all.*

*"I didn't go looking for answers," I said calmly. "They found me. I purposefully sat at the funeral and said I wanted to be able to look at you when asked who I could trust. And you said nothing! I said no more secrets, and you said nothing! You think I didn't notice your baggy clothes, your slow walks or you rubbing your belly, fat ass?"*

*Stephanie covered her mouth, her entire body stiff.*

*"I've had time to process," I continued. "To unravel. To rebuild."*

*I turned toward her, stepped closer, and whispered, "You think this ends with you?"*

*Stephanie's voice cracked. "Bianca… what are you saying?"*

*"I've already taken care of it."*

*Stephanie stepped back, nearly tripping over herself. "Taken care of what?"*

*I didn't answer. I just turned and grabbed my purse. Before stepping out, I looked back, my expression unreadable.*

*"Check your email when you get home."*

*Stephanie's hands were shaking. "Bianca, please…"*

*I tilted my head slightly. "Don't worry. This time, silence won't save you."*

*Stephanie's mouth fell open, but I walked out the door.*

## Chapter 21: PAINFUL MEMORY

"Stephanie, I had no idea you went through any of that. You were always here, on time, in class, ready to teach and learn. Have you spoken to Bianca since the funeral?"

"After the funeral, yes, at the memorial, but not after what she did, there was no way I could, but I don't want to talk any more about it. You said you would share something about yourself." As I wiped my tears from my face and sniffed the mucus that was attempting to shed.

I thought about what I had told Ms. Jefferies and started to replay every single memory in my head like a song on repeat. Every time I think about my past, it feels like a knife is cutting me in the middle of my chest. If I had one wish, it would be to start my life over in a way that I wanted it to be. More aligned with God's purpose and less of my plan.

"I'm listening, Mrs. Jefferies. I'm ready to learn more about you now."

## Chapter 22: AVOIDANCE

"Do you want to discuss what you did in email or__"

"NO!" I snapped, "Not right now. This has already been too much.

"Okay, can you tell me your plans for the journal you are holding? You kept it all this time, you must really care about it."

Holding the journal closer to my chest, "I do. She left this for me for a reason. She wanted me to know because she knew I needed closure. Tia wrote so much of her life here. I feel like I know her now more than I ever did. She was never the one to share her feelings with people.

"But now I know why," I added, "when you tell the truth, people either leave you, destroy you or destroy yourself. Then who can you trust after that? I stood, clutching the journal "so no, I'm not ready to discuss the email, not yet."

And I walked out.

# THANK YOU!

First and foremost, I want to thank my Heavenly Father for blessing me with the creativity, vision, and determination to bring this impactful, but relatable, story to life.

I began writing this book when I was just 18 years old. At the time, I knew I loved storytelling and dreamed of becoming a writer. This was one of the first stories I ever completed and copyrighted—and now, it's officially published. Yay, me!

To my family, friends, and loved ones, thank you for your endless support and encouragement, and for actually buying and reading the book—it means more than you know.

And to every reader who gave my book a chance: thank you from the bottom of my heart. Your time and attention are genuinely appreciated.

This is only the beginning!

A'Donna Renee

Made in the USA
Monee, IL
08 July 2025

20709331R00100